Between Black and Dark-Grey

Short Stories

Ewa Mazierska

Contents

Anita

It was one of the worst days in our lives when mother told me and Patrick that she was pregnant. We didn't want to have siblings; our house was too small even for its current inhabitants and we didn't have a father who would look after us – he was a drunkard, who disappeared from home for extended periods. We were like a family from a Thomas Hardy or D.H. Lawrence novel, except that we were born well into the end of the twentieth century. But it only made our predicament worse, as we felt that we were not only economically disadvantaged, but frozen in time. Another child would render us even more backward.

We were especially incensed by the fact that the pregnancy was planned by our mother – it was her ploy to keep our father at home. She assumed that he would take pity on her and give up his lover. Instead, upon learning that his wife got pregnant, our father left her for good. In due course, his lover kicked him out, but he still didn't return to his wife.

Mother must have been so despondent by this situation that she became distracted and careless, and one day she was hit by a car near our house in Chorley, whose driver run away. Subsequently she spent two months in hospital, while we were looked after by our aunt and social services, neither of whom we liked. This period made Patrick and me realise that things can always get worse. Lying in bed, we'd invent such situations. For example, Patrick died and I was on my own, or vice versa, or mother died in childbirth or survived, but returned home in a wheelchair. The child was disabled and mother was unable to look after her (by this point we knew that mother was expecting a daughter). We were put with two different foster families, and never saw each other again.

These stories did not reflect our natural penchant for omens or pessimism, but a need to prepare ourselves for whatever might happen in our lives. We also believed that once we invented the worst-case scenario, we would eliminate it from reality. But even without experiencing these situations, Patrick was miserable and once, in the middle of the night, he said: 'I can't live like this. I want to die.' But he didn't die. Being only ten, he didn't even know how to commit suicide. Moreover, I wanted him to carry on living, for his and my own sake. This was because I wouldn't have anybody left, if he died. By this point the new child didn't matter; we didn't treat her as one of us.

Yet, not everything was hopeless in our lives. We did well at school and had some friends, although because they were from better families, we kept them at a distance as we didn't want them to know about our situation. We were too proud to stand anybody's pity.

Eventually the child was born, six weeks prematurely. Mother decided to name her Anita. This wasn't a name she liked particularly, but she said that it was the name she was given by the woman who was in the car which hit her. Apparently, this woman didn't run away, as we thought, but left the car, put her hand on her belly and said 'Welcome Anita' – and only then drove away. I found the story bizarre and most likely a reflection of mother's trauma. I wanted my sister to be called Chloe, but mother was adamant that Anita was the right name for the newcomer and so Anita she was. The child and mother stayed in the hospital for almost a month after the birth, due to the poor health of both of them. We were told that it was a miracle that Anita survived as on two occasions it felt as if she crossed the line dividing life and death – the first time when mother was hit by the car and the second time when she was giving birth and Anita's heart stopped beating. Yet, on each occasion she pulled through. The male doctor told us this not to scare us, but to prepare us for the problems which we might have with our little sister – as if we didn't have enough problems without her.

When Patrick and I saw Anita for the first time, she looked thin, pale and sickly. According to Patrick, she looked like an alien, not a human being. But I thought she looked a bit like me and despite her poor state, there was a certain alertness about her. One could feel that she gazed at us with interest and even attempted a smile. This moved me. I kissed her and cuddled her and asked mother if I could carry Anita on the way home. Another reason why I wanted to do it was that I didn't trust mother. The accident, the effort of giving birth and the long period of hospitalisation made her weak and unfit to look after a baby. She even couldn't walk properly, but had a limp, and there was a danger that the baby would slip from her arms when her body leaned more to the limping side. Mother agreed and thus, even though I was only eight, I was the one who brought Anita to her new home and put her in her new bed, which was in fact an old bed – one used previously by Patrick and myself. The bed stayed in mother's bedroom, but she told me to 'sleep light', in case something happened to the girl.

Unlike me, Patrick didn't warm to our sister – he found her disgusting and a nuisance, and he regarded the whole situation embarrassing. Although he didn't say it, he was also jealous of the attention I was giving Anita. I told him that if we both looked after our little sister, this would bring us even closer together, but he disagreed. He kept saying that she came into our life to put a wedge between us.

'How can a defenceless baby come up with such a plan?' I asked, rhetorically, but he answered as if it was a proper question:

'She is not defenceless, I'm not even sure she is a baby,' he said, kicking the leg of the bed, as if he wanted to harm the child, but had no courage to do it.

'Stop it,' I said, crying, to which he reacted to by leaving the house.

In the first years of her existence Anita did not develop as normal children do. She ate very little, throwing up most of the food she was given, and grew little. Neither did her hair grow; she was bald and her nails were as delicate and transparent as thin plastic foil. The doctors and nurses pointed to two problems with our sister. One was the lack of iron, causing anaemia; another was a heart defect, which put her on the threshold of death. Often at night my mother would run into my room, telling me that Anita had died, and it seemed that way, as she was very cold and her heart had stopped beating. But when I brought her to my bed, took off her clothes and put her next to my body, she warmed up, her heart started to beat and her eyes opened up as if she was waking from a deep sleep. So mother used me more and more at night and eventually it was agreed that Anita and I would sleep together in one bed.

At two, Anita was still unable to walk or say more than five words. However, among those early words was my name, 'Eve', maybe because it was easy to say or because I was the one who was always checking on her and talking to her. When Anita grew a bit, she learnt to catch my hand over her bed and put it on her heart as if to reassure me that it worked well. By this point Patrick called our sister a 'retard' on the account of what she couldn't do, but I had a feeling that she wasn't lagging behind her peers; she just developed differently from them. Still, I felt like she lacked something, which prevented her from reaching her potential.

One day a neighbour came by with something in her bag. It turned out it to be a pig's heart. She said that she was in the countryside and was invited to attend the slaughtering of a pig at an organic farm. According to this new fashion, meat-eaters were encouraged to see animals being killed or even do it themselves rather than leaving this unpleasant task to illegal immigrants or the poor. The neighbour, who liked to be in tune with the times, did so and said it was fine for her to look at the dying pig: it went fast and smooth. What concerned her, however, was that so much of the meat was left to waste, as English people stopped eating many parts of the pig. It occurred to her to request the heart, thinking about our anaemic Anita, as she remembered that organ meat was an important source of iron. Our mother looked on in dismay at the piece wrapped in the blood-soaked paper, as she herself never ate any offal, but I said: 'Let's give it a try. It wouldn't harm Anita. If she won't like it, she will throw it up.'

We cut two small pieces of the heart and of those one I fried in olive oil and the other I stewed with butter and some milk. I cut the cooked meat into small pieces and waited till it was the right temperature before offering it to Anita. To our surprise, she ate everything and wanted more, so I cooked her more, even though my mother was worried that so much food would kill her, given how little she ate normally. By the time she went to sleep, she ate half of the pig's heart.

The next day she ate the rest of the heart and so we started to feed her organ meat. By this time, I was myself vegetarian, soon to become vegan and people who stuffed themselves with meat repulsed me. But not Anita, because I felt that she gorged on meat not out of greed, but of necessity. And I was proven right. In the year when she was given the hearts and livers of animals, she learnt to walk and talk. Our conversations during this period were simple, but contained ideas which were unusual for a child of Anita's age. Most importantly, she understood that sleep was similar to death and she asked me to wake her up when she was about to die. When I asked her how to do it, she showed me my heart – it was my heart which was meant to put her heart into movement, give her life.

At this point my brother stopped calling Anita 'retard' and started to call her 'cannibal'. It was meant to be a joke, but I didn't find it funny. Anita didn't call him names in revenge, but didn't use his name either. For her Patrick was 'he'.

Because of her strange food preferences, weak heart and the sense that she was a child like no other, mother and I were reluctant to send Anita to the nursery, but eventually the decision was made for her to go, as mother needed a full-time job to feed and clothe us. She also needed to leave home, because at home she felt entrapped.

The nursery teachers lacked the time or intelligence to see how unusual Anita was. They only noticed that she was a 'shy child', that she 'kept herself to herself', but this was okay because there were many kids like her in this respect. They also mentioned that she ate little and often fell asleep, paradoxically not when there was peace in the room, but when there was the greatest noise, and her sleep was very deep.

I was worried that due to being so idiosyncratic and unsocial, my sister might be bullied by the other children, so I tried to explain to her that she needed to stay on good terms with her peers. This was unnecessary, as Anita understood it herself. She learnt to imitate and blend in with the other kids, without being truly involved with them. And the other kids liked her, because she was very good in games and solving problems, yet not competitive or aggressive.

Anita didn't mind the nursery apart from her hunger. Mother asked if it would be possible to cook offal for Anita in the nursery or microwave meat she cooked herself, but both requests were rejected on the grounds of food safety and creating a precedence which would lead to providing a hundred kids with a hundred different meals and thus adding to the workload of already overworked dinner ladies. To cut Anita's suffering mother and I tried to collect Anita earlier from the nursery. Although I was myself only a child, I was allowed to do so and Anita preferred if it was me who brought her home. This was because we had much to talk about and I allowed her to eat uncooked meat and didn't restrict its amount. I found my way to an abattoir where I bought a lot of offal for very little money from Eastern European workers who liked to sell things on the side. To afford it, I earned extra money doing errands for our elderly neighbours.

By the time she was three, Anita had caught up with her peers in terms of size. When she started primary school, she was taller than most girls in her class. She was also more inquisitive. She wanted to know why life was based on killing; why people couldn't be like the gods or angels who populated the books in the Catholic school she attended, who were born without any material urges,.I replied that such creatures existed only in the human imagination; real living things were part of a food chain.

'Who made the world this way?' she asked.

'It made itself, most likely,' I replied.

'No,' she said. 'There must be god

'Most likely there is no god', I replied.'Can we change the world so we don't need to kill?'

'Maybe, but better leave things as they are and look the other way.'

This is what I tried to do when visiting abattoirs, but it did not work that well. Straight after such visits I was sick and at night I had dreams about plunging knives into the throats or hearts of pigs which fell on me with their heavy bodies. And such dreams were nothing in comparison with what happened later.

When Anita was nine, a child was murdered in the school toilet. The hypothesis was that the perpetrator entered the school undetected, did his gruesome deed and then left, again without attracting anybody's attention. But I knew it was Anita.

'Why did you do it?' I asked her, when this information became public.

'I was very hungry and angry, and couldn't control myself,' she said.

There wasn't much remorse in her voice; it felt as if she was just stating the fact.

'How did you do it?' I asked, although I didn't really want to know.

'With a knife.'

This information suggested that Anita had prepared herself for her act, which on one hand scared me even more, but on the other hand suggested that she was aware of the danger of being caught and took the necessary precautions.

'You don't need to kill people,' I said to her. 'You can eat animal offal, as before. I can get more of it for you,' I said.

'You will have to work yourself to death to get me as much food as I need, and I need what is warm and hasn't been re-heated,' she said with a smile, satisfied with her ability to use cryptic language, which she most likely got from me. 'Besides, you told me yourself to do what I want to and look the other way'.

Seeing me sulking, she added: 'Better kill me than make me starve. But I assure you I won't do it at school again. It's too dangerous. I couldn't breathe in this toilet out of fear. And when it was over, I peed myself and had to throw away my pants and tights.'

'Hopefully you haven't left them in the toilet', I said.

'No, I put in a plastic bag and left in a bin near the market.' I couldn't kill my sister, but I hoped to contain Anita's murderous urges, in the same way Dexter's father from the famous American series was able to channel his son's need for blood. The thought that I would have to devote my life to this task was comforting, because it meant being liberated from other pursuits which, I expected, would bring me frustration and most likely be futile, such as having a family of my own.

The most important thing was to ensure that that Anita remained safe, when following her affliction. Hence, we agreed that she wouldn't kill anybody from Chorley or even Preston. The closest acceptable place she could go in search for victims was Manchester, but she didn't like Manchester, claiming that the city was 'too open'. Blackpool was ideal, but being socially-minded, she decided to leave Blackpool in peace, as she didn't want to ruin its fragile economy. Hence, she kept going to

Lancaster and York, before she moved her operations to London, where her deeds disappeared in the sea of what was labelled 'knife crime'.

Several years after Anita's first 'accident', I chose to study serology, to get access to blood banks, thinking that human blood was what really Anita was after. My sister, however, was dismissive: 'I'm after prey, not just blood. You couldn't do anything about it. But maybe you can find out why I am the way I am.'

This was, however, difficult. The answer, for sure, wasn't in Anita's blood, as she had 0+, the most common blood group in the UK. Maybe it was in the experience of other people with family members like our sister.

The internet was already in existence when I started to enquire, but people did not advertise that they had vampires at home, most likely in fear of losing them. So, as a substitute, I joined clubs for families searching for help with dealing with violent children. However, such meetings only confirmed my suspicion that Anita was nothing like an ordinary psychopath. I was also put off by the ease with which these people disowned their relatives, seeking the most feeble excuses to claim that they did not truly belong to their families, and the pressure to open up, which I resisted the greater the pressure. After several months I gave up, accepting that I would never find out the truth. Still, I never lost interest in Anita's condition, trying to read everything what was available about vampires, past and present. One thing which I learnt was that the ascent of a vampire marked the break of the social order. The vampire, even if him or herself was not a revolutionary, marked the ascent of the revolution. However, in England at the time there was no sign or even talk of a revolution, only the woolly 'greens' talked about a need for a green revolution, yet without offering anything practical.

Paradoxically, once my brother discovered Anita's true nature, he warmed to her. He provided her with the first knife, as she needed one which only adults could buy. He was even proud of her, because she wasn't a weakling like our mother or me. When Anita left home for her he sat at home, drinking red wine, as if he wanted to salute her or even imagined himself accompanying her. He told me that thanks to Anita he felt more self-confident, even invincible, as if he suffered from Munchausen Syndrome. He also suggested that I should bask in our sister's dark glory, because Anita made all of us special.

It turned out that Patrick was more of the 'Dexter's father' in relation to Anita than me, as he directed her to potential victims: paedophiles, members of grooming gangs, drug dealers and rich people, who in his view deserved to die. He identified the spots where she could meet them – the rest depended on Anita. The important thing was to meet them one on one, because she was only a girl, even though she was tall and strong as for her age.

Her task was to kill them quickly, suck their blood and free them of their valuables. It was Patrick who exchanged the jewellery, watches and mobile phones for cash; they typically didn't do anything about the credit cards. The earnings weren't huge, but allowed Patrick and Anita to go through the university without taking any jobs or maintenance loans and made them look comfortably middle class. On a couple of occasions when the booty was significant: more than twenty thousand pounds, they put it in the bank. They suggested that I share in their profit, but I refused to do it, as I didn't want to have 'blood on my hands'. On reflection, it was a stupid thing to do, because, metaphorically speaking, I had almost as much blood on my hands as Patrick, and my aloofness drew a wedge between me and my siblings. While I shared their worries, I was left out of their joy, consisting, for example, of learning the identities of Anita's victims, which were often revealed in the news, together with wrong explanations of their deaths, which immensely amused them, till they got used to the ineptness and lack of the imagination of the British police. Typically, the deaths were attributed to turf wars and personal conflicts, while in fact it was Anita's interventions which led to subsequent turf wars and personal vendettas.

It never occurred to the investigators that there was something highly unnatural in the paleness of these victims, perhaps because a large proportion of them were brown, black or mixed race. In relation to these crimes, the police visited us only once. It happened when our father was found dead. In this case, however, neither of us was regarded as a suspect; we were simply asked if we knew anybody who could hold any grudges against him, given that he had some debts. His death, besides, was different to those of Anita's other victims. She let him die slowly and didn't drink his blood, finding him too disgusting to dismember. There was, however, one case, when we were traced by a relative of Anita's victim: a sister of a drug dealer. This man, whose name was Tom, took Anita's photo in a bar and it was the last photo on his phone and, indeed, the last trace of his activities. For some reason the police ignored it and the resourceful woman decided to trace Anita on her own. Although by this point the technologies of facial recognition were in their infancy, and I couldn't imagine a different way of uncovering Anita's identity, the girl, named Sophia, succeeded and one day arranged to meet her.

I decided to be present at the meeting, even though I knew that my sister had enough intelligence to handle the situation. Indeed, she told Sophia that she and Tom parted ways before having sex and that most likely he had another meeting afterwards which proved deadly. Sophia appeared to accept this explanation, but later she kept stalking me, asking me questions about Anita. She managed to discover that my sister was linked to two more violent deaths: that of our father and a girl in her class. After a year or so, when I asked her to leave us in peace, she caught me at work and told me that she knew it was Anita who killed her brother and it was my duty to report her to the police – otherwise more people would suffer. After this encounter we had a family council and decided that Sophia needed to disappear too. Anita took care of this assignment. However, she did not use Sophia as nourishment, as we wanted her death to be as different from the death of her brother as possible, and also for her to die as dignified a death as the circumstances allowed.

Needless to add, it was distressing to see somebody who cared so much about Anita's victim and learn that this victim was an extremely nice, harmless and talented young man with a life ahead of him. However, being a relative of a vampire means that there is no time for sentimentality, and hypocrisy is something I always loathed.

Several months after Sophia's death Anita moved to Australia, where she got a job at a university, as a lecturer in chemistry. I assumed that she went so far away to prevent me from monitoring her life and also not to cause me extra worry. But instead I worried all the time, about all these people who were my sister's prey and about her being caught. Carrying this secret made me wary of people. I felt like I couldn't be close to anybody because I couldn't share this secret with anyone, yet without sharing it I couldn't be intimate and I would stay lonely. For Patrick this wasn't a problem. He even enjoyed the fact that, except for his blood family (he pronounced the word 'blood' in a special way, to point to its double meaning and make a joke with it), nobody knew who we really were; it gave him power over his friends and girlfriends especially. In fact, he was so proud to have a vampire sister that on occasion he hinted at this fact, making me anxious that somebody would eventually decide to investigate. Yet, nothing like that ever happened; Patrick's friends took him for a joker.

Anita's departure to Australia also affected our mother. While throughout Anita's childhood and teenage years she avoided her youngest daughter, aware that she wasn't in a position to look after her, once she was out of her sight, she invented stories which were meant to prove she was a good mother to her and they enjoyed each other's company. The longer Anita was living abroad, the closer mother felt to her. To strengthen this narrative, she even attributed to me Anita's certain characteristics and vice versa. I became the one who was very fussy about food, while my sister was the one who ate everything which was put on the table, even humble haggis and trotters. On occasion, and especially when her health was ailing, she also mused on the accident during her pregnancy, telling me how much she suffered from it and prayed to save the injured child, although I knew that this was a blatant lie – Anita's survival was a nuisance for mother. The only thing which was of interest to me was that the more time was passing, the more she remembered the accident and claimed that one of the two women who left the car looked like Anita.

Anita was reluctant to return to England and neither did she want us to visit her. Besides, for mother and me it was difficult, because in her old age mother was unable to leave home and I was looking after her.

Yet, there were situations when Anita felt obliged to return. One of them was Patrick's wedding; another was the birth of his first child: a boy named Alan, who was lovely, but caused me to mourn doubly all these lovely boys and girls whom my brother and myself prevented from being conceived. Anita didn't stay for long, though, citing a situation at her work as a reason to return. I knew, however, that it was hunger which she didn't want to quench in England, which made her hurry. I tried not to quiz her about her lifestyle, but once I couldn't resist and asked her how did she found her prey.

'In Australia it's easy. There's plenty of space, plenty of people walking without a purpose, tourists and locals, waiting for something interesting to happen. So I happen to them and I feel as if they are happy about our encounter. Sometimes I tell them: "I'm blood-thirsty. Will you be able to satisfy me?' and they say "Yes" and you know what happens next. People there are also juicier and their blood tastes better – it's enough for me to hunt once a month and not to go hungry. They also have better knives – the best in the world.'

'That's great,' I said, even though I knew this word was inappropriate.

The next time Anita came was for mother's funeral. Although the occasion was sombre and the weather was a typical wet, cloudy

Northern English spring, we had a good time. I felt like I finally 'reclaimed' my sister. She slept with me in my old bed, clutching to my back and I heard her heart beating in its typical irregular way, stopping from time to time.

Before she returned to Australia, I came across an article on a website called 'New Science', a space for renegade scientists and charlatans, as its very title suggested, which I nevertheless consumed avidly. Its title was 'HIV and Vampire Virus as a Response to Overpopulation'. Its author, from the United States, had come up with the theory that the AIDS epidemic was a response of some responsible scientists to the threat of overpopulation and in the last instance destruction of humanity. AIDS was a contagious illness which was meant to wipe out large swathes of the world, as was the case before with the plague. But it did not happen, because the disease was so public – at some stage everybody was talking about it and huge resources were put into containing it. So a new virus was introduced, which the author described as a 'vampire virus'. People who got it needed the blood of fellow humans, but also a certain way to access it – by drinking it directly from the body. In a nutshell, they became murderers, which is something the sick and their families kept to themselves. Moreover, the cases of vampirism were mis-diagnosed, mostly being attributed to ordinary crimes, hence preventing seeking a cure. Unlike AIDS, the illness spread discreetly, causing a triple reduction of lives: of the vampires themselves, who usually died before reaching thirty,, their victims and those to whom they passed on their virus. I was curious how the virus was passed, but this was meant to be published in the follow-up article which, however, was not published.

Shivers went through my spine as I was reading it. I was thinking about contacting the author, but there was no affiliation or an e-mail address. Obviously, he wrote this piece incognito. Maybe he was himself member of the group of these dark scientists, concerned about climate change, who decided to break rank. I wondered whether I should tell

Anita about this, as she always wanted to know how and why she became a vampire, but something prevented me from doing this.

The next time when Anita came, she was in no hurry to return. She said that she took a leave of absence from her work to recuperate and she wanted to stay with me longer, maybe as long as a year. I knew what it meant – she would have to hunt. This thought freaked me out but I didn't say anything, as the pleasure of having her at home was greater than any negative feelings I had.

For the first two weeks of her stay I also took a holiday so we could travel together: to the Yorkshire Dales, the Lake District and the Peak District. She said that only in Australia did she realise that she never learned about England. She only knew Chorley and London.

When we were returning from one such trip a woman run in front of my car and I hit her. I jumped out and noticed with relief that I haven't killed her. Indeed, she appeared to be unharmed, although was shocked. I also noticed that she was pregnant.

'We must take you to the hospital,' I said, to which she said nothing, only looked at me with empty eyes.

'Leave her,' said Anita. 'She will be fine,' and then she put her hand on the belly of the woman and said to what was inside her: 'Welcome Chloe. Be brave!'

I knew that it was wrong to leave this woman like that, but had no strength to refuse Anita. When we were driving away, I noticed that my sister was getting pale, but not in her usual glowing way, but yellowish-ashy. Her breathing became weaker and once we reached home, she didn't have enough strength to leave the car. I thus carried her in my arms, surprised how light she was. She reminded me of the day when I brought her home from the hospital, shortly after she was born. I took off our clothes and put her body on top of me, so that our hearts could meet, as I did when Anita was a child. But this didn't help; within minutes she died. I started to cry and was crying for hours, not sure whether more out of sorrow of losing Anita or losing my purpose in life. But then it occurred to me that in couple of months somewhere not far from my home a pale and sick child would be born. Should I seek the little Chloe or let fate decide about her future? I still have several weeks to make up my mind.

A Bargain

Andrew had an eye for a bargain, especially damaged goods, whose defects were more than balanced by a reduction in their price. Nicole thought that she was also a bargain for him, given that he courted her when she was at the most vulnerable stage of her life, following a breakdown and a stint in a psychiatric hospital. However, she didn't discuss this, as she didn't really want him to know the truth.

The other bargains they talked about all the time because, well, finding a bargain seemed to be Andrew's main pursuit. Previously, however, these were smaller things, with a car bought at a discount being the largest; but now they were ready to hunt for a house and, of course, it had to be a bargain, because prices were high and most of young people were expected to live with their parents till their parents' or their own death. For several months they browsed the internet, trying to find something at a reduced price, which looked acceptable, but without success.

Then they decided to visit estate agents and they found themselves in an office of a man who had an award for selling the largest number of properties in Scotland the previous year.

After looking at the houses advertised in his window, which were either ugly or beyond their price range, Andrew asked: 'Maybe you have something like, you know, in *The Shining*: a house built on the graveyard of some wronged indigenous tribe?'

The agent, who looked intelligent and genuinely friendly, replied: 'Literally we don't have such a house, but we might have something which approaches your requirement.'

'What is it?', asked Andrew.

'It's a house which an eminent Scottish architect, Paul S., received as part of his payment for designing a small housing estate some twenty miles from here, on the headland, overseeing the North Sea at its most picturesque. However, the project was marred by problems – the villagers living below the estate considered this land as their own and they regarded those who bought the new houses as trespassers. It also turned out that the estate was built too close to the shore according to the regulations, which were introduced just before the construction started. There were other irregularities, plus a banking crisis. Meaning people who paid for their new houses couldn't sell them and lost their investment. Many went bankrupt and some committed suicide: this was the hottest suicide spot for the whole of Scotland in that year. Mr. S. felt responsible for this unfortunate situation, given that many people chose to live there, lured by his name, which was used in all promotional materials. Although he used his savings to compensate the victims, it wasn't enough – blood was already spilled and his reputation in tatters, although wrongly, in my opinion.'

'Yes, I've read about it', said Nicole. 'I remember that some journalists compared it to the wave of suicides, following Hitler's death. There was one family who killed their three kids, like Mrs. Goebbels did.'

The estate agent made a face which conveyed his disapproval of such comparison, but Nicole continued, undeterred: 'It's amazing that something like that happened in Scotland. I always assumed that people here are protected, the state cares about them, unlike in England or anywhere in the world. This was a reason I chose to study and live in Scotland.'

'Well, banks are the same all of over the world and, when they fall, ordinary people have to pick up the buck', said the agent. 'But all of this is history now, it's well over a decade since these unfortunate events. By now, all these troubled houses have found new owners, except this one. This isn't because it is substandard, far from it. Indeed it's probably the best house on the estate, but until recently Mr. S.'s nephew, who is his heir, didn't want to sell it. It was only a week ago that he contacted me, saying that he had changed him mind. The only problem is that the property was never cleared after Mr. S.' death, apparently because the nephew wanted to do some research there on his uncle's architectural ideas. The owner will not charge you for any furniture or other items you wish to keep, in case you decide to buy it, but he won't pay you for getting rid of the rest or any damage which may have happened during the period when it was empty. And, I must say, the asking price is very attractive.'

'Sounds like a bargain', said Andrew, upon hearing it.

'It does not only sound it, it *is* a bargain', said the agent. 'In fact, the house hasn't gone on the market yet, but if you are seriously interested, I can show it to you tomorrow. You seem to be a nice young couple and I want to help the young as they have so much harder life than the older generations.'

Nicole was thinking that the agent didn't look much older than Andrew, but maybe such talk was part of the estate agent's manner of speaking.

*

Two days later Andrew and Nicole went to see the house. Although it was only fourteen years old, it felt old. In part this was due to neglect, and in part due to its design. It had many rooms of strange shapes, its walls were thick for a modern house and the windows were small, which made them look like eyes. Nicole was uneasy seeing such windows, as they felt too human to her. She took a towel from a bathroom and collected the moisture from their frames as she knew how unpleasant it was not being able to dry one's tears. Suddenly the sun reflected on the window pane, as if the house opened its eyes and wanted to thank Nicole for her care. She smiled, which was noticed by the agent.

'Great view, isn't it?', he asked, rhetorically. 'It's not a castle, but it feels like a castle, at the edge of the headland, surrounded by houses where the serfs live. Whoever chooses to dwell here, will feel like a king overlooking his subjects from one side and gazing into his freedom from another. All of lifes' situations are covered', he finished, laughing.

Nicole had to admit that one couldn't find a better location, with its views, being very private and, at the same time, close to the railway station and shops in the nearby village, situated below the headland.

'Except that it didn't work like that for its first owner', said Nicole.

'Yes and no, given that Mr. S. threw himself from the cliff – he thus chose his freedom', said the agent with a pinch of sarcasm, indicating his exasperation with Nicole's negative attitude.

'I've read that his body was never found', said Nicole.

'True, but somebody in the village saw him jumping. The thing about the sea is that it normally does not give back what we throw into it. Anyway, if Mr. S. wanted to claim his property, he had over ten years to do so.'

'It will work for us', said Andrew.

'Take your time', said the agent. 'I can keep it for a week for you, as I need to prepare it for putting on the market.'

When they returned home, Nicole said: 'I don't want to buy this house. First, we don't need such a big house, given that we want one child at most. It will be expensive to heat it. Second, there is something unsettling about it.'

'Of course, there is something unsettling about this house, so our task is to settle it, make it our own. Isn't it what you said before - that you don't want just to buy the house for *living*, but for *dwelling*, as put by your favourite philosopher', said Andrew.

'I don't know if I would be ever able to dwell there. Even living might be a bit of a challenge', replied Nicole.

'Be reasonable – there is nothing wrong with this house. It's large, stylish, comfortable and, most importantly, it's bargain, pure and simple. We have to buy it – it is a once in a lifetime opportunity. Happiness is easy. Life's what you make it.'

Nicole didn't like the fact that, when they were discussing serious matters, Andrew would use quotes to leverage his position; as if his own arguments wouldn't be believable in his own words, which made Nicole even more reluctant to trust him.

'Okay, but if something goes wrong, don't blame me', said Nicole.

'I won't', replied Andrew.

*

When the agent was giving them the key, he mentioned that Paul S.' nephew asked to return to him the owner's diary, in case they found it. Justine promised to do so – although she thought that not before reading it herself.

Although the house was a bargain, after paying a deposit and the fees to the lawyer and estate agent, Andrew and Nicole had hardly any money left; so there was no chance to buy any new furniture. They didn't even have money to go on a holiday, so decided to have a stay-cation, which wasn't a problem, given that moving to a new place felt like going on a vacation, especially in Summer, which was their case. Andrew suggested that once they had savings again, they would get rid of the old stuff and buy new furniture, perhaps with the assistance of an interior designer. The alternative was to sell them on gumtree or e-bay one by one, gradually replacing the old pieces with new ones. The danger of such an approach was that they would end up with the hodgepodge of the sort which the previous owner had left them.

Nicole's view was that they should wait till they had significantly more money, because it would be difficult to get rid of the old furniture the way Andrew suggested. Although the taste of the previous owner was eclectic, and each piece of furniture belonged to a different period, there was a certain logic to their arrangement, hence getting rid of one piece would destroy the balance. It felt as the furniture didn't just sit there but directed the inhabitant from one room to the next. Moreover, it encouraged them to rest, which Nicole found comforting, even liberating, given that Andrew was perpetually busy and restless and even regarded restlessness as his moral duty. Nicole never saw so many easy and chaise lounge chairs in one house. She wondered when the architect was working if he was always relaxing. But she discovered that he was in fact working while resting, as proved by various contraptions attached to these chairs, whose purpose was to extend them so that they changed into office spaces with stands and attachments to put papers of different sizes on. There were three chairs which reflected what Nicole's thoughts were regarding the different stages of Paul's states of concentration. Nicole also remembered that when they entered the house for the first time, the chairs were in a particular order, with the most 'workable' located furthest from windows and the most relaxing being next to the bay window. The days when she was at home, she followed this order and noticed that, using them in this way, she never felt tired or stressed. Even the following day, when she went to work, nothing put her off-balance. There was also one chair, placed in front of the wall, and the adjacent part of the wall there seemed a bit lighter than the rest, as if the paint had peeled off or faded, but she regarded it as a sign of the chair being moved, maybe by an estate agent.

In addition to furniture, Paul left crockery, cutlery, and pictures on the walls. As with his furniture, nothing was in proper sets. It felt like he never bought anything on purpose, but just tried to put the things which he found into use. In order not to create more clutter, Nicole moved some of their own things to the loft which was full of Paul's boxes.

Many of these boxes had names of places where he had worked: Mexico, Chile, California, Lithuania and Poland, as well as Dorset and Somerset. The estate agent told them that, prior to this development, he designed many estates near the seaside, all over the world, and his designs were known for going against the grain. His houses were not the typical kitschy seaside villas with thin walls, large windows and flat roofs, but solid buildings with thick walls, small windows and sloping roofs, like eighteenth century fishermen's cottages. This was because he expected the temperature outside to rise over the next century and the houses would serve more as an escape from heat, not only in hot places, but also temperate ones. Paul also claimed that small windows provide a better view of the sea, as they make the inhabitants gaze rather than just look. But this was all the estate agent knew about his architectural ideas.

Shortly after moving in, Nicole learnt that somebody at Edinburgh University had written a Master's thesis about Paul S.'s architectural style. The person in charge of the university repository told her that she could consult it on the premises, as the thesis wasn't digitised. Unfortunately, it was based only on secondary sources and with theory overwhelming any insights about Paul's actual work. This made her eager to undertake her own inquiry. Nicole engaged in her research only when Andrew was at work, which meant just one day per week, as that was all she had free – Wednesday. She didn't want to rummage in the loft in Andrew's presence, because she regarded her work in the attic to be private. There was another reason she preferred to do it on her own – a couple of weeks after they moved in, Andrew started to suffer from a cough and attributed it to dust which had accumulated in the house when it was uninhabited. Nicole tried to convince him that there was no dust, as she was cleaning the house regularly, and not only vacuuming , but using a mop, but Andrew insisted that the dust lay deeper. When his coughing worsened, he claimed that it wasn't just dust, but dust worms, proliferating in a dusty environment:

'They penetrated the floors and the walls over the years and now are climbing to the surface, encouraged by the light and warmth. When they are let in, they never leave and now they are copulating with sea worms coming in here through the windows. In no time at all, we will have here super-worms: super-vicious and cunning, like super-rats, attacking New York.'

To prove it, Andrew went to the window and put his finger into the window frame, to show Nicole the mud which accumulated there. When he was doing so, Nicole noticed a greenish circle appearing in the middle of the window, as if it was a pupil observing what was going on inside.

'What you say doesn't make sense. There are no super-worms', said Nicole. 'Anyway, what do you propose?', she asked.

He didn't say anything, as it was Andrew's idea to buy this house and they didn't have an option to move out. A week later he visited a doctor who confirmed that he had a breathing problem, gave him some medicine and advised him to take walks on the shore, as seaside air was a perfect medicine for curing asthma.

Whilst Andrew's breathing worsened, Nicole felt that hers improved. This resulted from being less stressed and having the right temperature in the house. It wasn't due to switching on or not switching on the heating, as they hadn't using it yet, given that they moved-in in April, but because the temperature in the house was changing according to her needs. Whenever she entered the house, returning from work, warm air surrounded her like a cocoon and kept her like that till she settled somewhere and then it thinned and the whole room became pleasantly warm. The cocoon returned when she was leaving the house, as if it wanted to prevent her from the shock of the changing temperature or just to make her aware that somebody at home cared about her. For sure, it wasn't Andrew, who became more callous by the day. The same changes concerned their sleep. Andrew, who used to fall asleep a minute after a shag, now lay awake for hours and, when he eventually got to sleep, he was sighing, snoring, and squirming in the bed, as if trying to crush his internal demons. Nicole cowered in her corner of bed and, increasingly, moved to sleep in another room. It seemed like Andrew didn't mind this, being completely preoccupied with his ailing health.

*

It was a couple of months after moving-in when Nicole properly met her neighbour. This was, in part, because they didn't have neighbours nearby, living some distance from the rest of the estate. But, one day, a woman in her thirties stopped when Nicole was working in the garden to say 'Hello'.

'Hello', replied Nicole.

'I'm Andrea. I live with my husband George on this estate, the first house from you on the left. I've noticed that you moved here with your partner. We were very curious to meet you. I hope you didn't mean me being so nosy.'

'No, not at all. It's understandable', said Nicole. 'Everybody wants to know their neighbours. I wondered whether we should introduce ourselves, but apparently people have stopped doing this, and we also thought that, given that we live some distance from the rest of the estate, we don't have proper neighbours. I'm Nicole, by the way.'

'I didn't come here to reproach you. I'm here to ask whether you like it here?', said Andrea.

'I do like it here very much. There is plenty of space for us and the view of the sea is magnificent. How about you?'

'Difficult to say', said Andrea. 'The houses on the estate are well built, but they have a peculiar atmosphere. You heard that this is a "suicide estate" – there was a year where more people committed suicide on this estate alone than in the rest of Scotland put together.'

'I know, but it was some time ago', said Nicole.

'True, but these things are not easily forgotten. People also say that some of these suicides weren't really suicides – they were murders by proxy.'

'What do you mean by that?', asked Nicole.

'I mean that people technically committed suicide, but on behest of higher powers, so to speak', replied Andrea in a whisper, despite the fact that nobody in this place could overhear them.

'Is that not the case with all suicides? People hear a "call" to do it', asked Nicole, slightly mischievously.

'It's not what I mean', replied Andrea. 'The gossip has it that since people moved here, they became a subject of different forces. The architect who designed this estate was aware of them, therefore he installed himself in the middle, to keep these forces in check, but they overpowered him. He was practically murdered', said Andrea in a conspiratorial tone.

'That's impossible', said Nicole. 'He jumped off the cliff.'

'If it was a suicide, why didn't he leave any suicide note or a will? And most importantly, why his body was never found?' asked Andrea.

'Maybe he didn't care what would happen after his death. As for his body disappearing, this happens when people drown in the sea. It is more difficult to find the bodies than to not find them.'

'He wasn't somebody who didn't care', replied Andrea. 'Some people said that the opposite was the case – he held meetings with residents to prepare them for his departure.'

'If you are so certain that he was murdered, what is your hypothesis?', asked Nicole.

'I don't have one, but I'm sure something is wrong again.'

'Maybe you shouldn't have bought your house, if you were so superstitious', said Nicole, feeling almost angry at her neighbour.

'I didn't want to buy it, but George insisted that we go ahead. He was tired of looking and failing to accomplish a transaction. He wanted us to settle and have a child. And now we cannot conceive. George wants us to have IVF treatment, but I'm worried. I prefer to wait, as my instinct tells me that it's not a good time and place to have a child.'

'Why you think so?'

'Well, George has been restless since we moved here and recently he does not feel well. He has a dry cough and cannot sleep at night, worried that he will suffocate and die in his sleep.'

'Has he been to the doctor?'

'He has, but the doctor couldn't find anything specific. He said it must be flu and asked him to take time off from work and measure his temperature every day.'

'And does he do that?'

'Yes, but his health doesn't improve, it only makes him more exasperated.'

'Do you know when his coughing started?'

'About a month ago. Why do you ask?'

'Just out of curiosity', replied Nicole.

*

Nicole was wondering whether she should tell Andrew about her talk with Andrea, but decided to keep quiet about it, as it would only confirm his prejudices against their house. Luckily, Andrew felt better after returning to work, where he noticed that he was not alone with having a cough. It felt like every second colleague was coughing in their office, which was strange, given the time of the year. Men seemed to be more affected by this ailment than women. In comparison with his work pals, he felt more robust. This also made him better disposed to their house because, rather than assuming that he caught his illness at home, he came to the conclusion that he brought it home from work.

Two more weeks had passed and one of the guys he worked with, died. Admittedly, he was one of the oldest in his office and wasn't a paragon of health, being overweight and a smoker before quitting in his fifties. His death shocked the workforce, especially two female colleagues and Andrew took upon himself the task of consoling them, often going to pubs with them before returning home. Nicole didn't mind as she enjoyed her solitude, as the house became her favoured companion.

Another couple of weeks passed and Nicole found an article in an Edinburgh newspaper about the rise in respiratory illnesses in Scotland's capital and the region of Fife. The same day some Scottish government minister was interviewed about the topic on television and, in typical fashion, he blamed the English, arguing that they smuggled the virus with their other dirty stuff. He even threatened to close the borders. This caused a rift with Westminster; the Prime Minister said that closing borders would only benefit the English who didn't have any problems with breathing. The spat lasted a week or so. During this time over fifty Scottish people died from the mysterious virus, almost exclusively men, giving the illness an unofficial name of the 'Scottish flu', which made the Scottish government furious.

Nicole was curious if any of the dead had lived on their estate and decided to find out, starting with Andrea. She went to her house, enquiring about George's health. Andrea was touched by her concern, replying that luckily her husband recovered. She also informed Nicole that there were several other cases of the 'Scottish flu' on the estate, but none was serious. In contrast to the estate, three people from the neighbouring village had died. Although Andrea pretended to be concerned about these deaths, Nicole felt that in reality the opposite was the case, as she didn't like these pesky villagers, who never came to terms with outsiders occupying the territory which they regarded as their own, although metaphorically and literally they lived 'below them', like rats on a ship waiting for their hosts to get weak, so they could attack them.

'How did this illness emerge in Scotland?', asked Nicole.

'I don't know. Most likely somebody brought it in from abroad.'

'But from where?'

'Nobody knows at this point. No other country has admitted to having the virus. But the government wants to check all people who arrived from abroad in the last three months.'

Nicole sighed with relief that they weren't in this category.

'What if it is home-grown, if it came from the sea, for example?', she asked.

'I don't think it's possible. Viruses need to live on people or animals to survive. But I'm not a virologist. I'm curious how the Scottish government will handle it. They always like to put blame on others, when something goes wrong in Scotland and, usually, they get away with doing so, but it might not be so easy this time. People are dying in growing numbers and their families want answers.'

'Well, it will be good to have answers, so we can feel safe', said Nicole.

*

Back in the house, Nicole sat next to a window, as she did after returning home from work, touching the glass with her hands, except that that day she hadn't returned from work, but hadn't been, instead telling her boss that she might have caught the mysterious illness. Nobody wanted it, so she was told to state at home until any symptoms of illness disappeared, and she promised to do so.

As always, the window was wet and tinged yellow, but the colour was more intense than when they moved in and the liquid collected in the edges was slightly oily. The house was really living, but not exactly in the way she initially thought. However, she had no time to ponder on this, as she had to cook dinner for her and Andrew. As soon as she put potatoes and vegetables in the oven, there was a call.

'I'm sorry to disturb you. I guess I'm speaking to Nicole. I'm Jonathan, a nephew of the previous owner of your house.'

'Yes, I know. The estate agent told us that you live in New Zealand.'

'That'scorrect. In fact, my father emigrated so far in order to be away from his brother.'

'I didn't know that.'

'Yes, they became distant, first figuratively and then also literally. But my family's history isn't a reason why I'm contacting you. I'm phoning to ask you if you found out, by any chance, my uncle's diary. I mentioned it to the estate agent that you can keep everything except for this one item.'

'I know, but I couldn't find it, although I went through his boxes. Looks like his entire archive from the last three years or so of your uncle's life disappeared: architectural notes, designs, photos. Maybe he was so unhappy that he destroyed it.'

'I don't think it was his style. More likely somebody took it.'

'Who would do that? The house wasn't burgled.'

'It could be one of his friends or collaborators.'

'Sorry to ask you, but why are you phoning just now?'

'I've read that a deadly virus appeared in Fife and it occurred to me that it might have something to do with my uncle.'

'How come?'

'I know this sounds crazy, but after he got into trouble with the estate, he was so angry that he planned revenge. He teamed up with some virologist who was working on long-living viruses. His idea was to plant such a virus into his house so that it infected its inhabitants who would then take the germ out into the world. This was in fact a version of his larger idea of designing "living houses": houses which would adjust to their owners not only in a metaphorical sense, but also literally.'

'How would that happen?'

' I don't know. If I knew, I would design such a house myself.'

'I think I've read somewhere about such houses, but it was stuff of science fiction, not science.'

'Yes, but my uncle kept saying that fifty percent of science fiction becomes science within fifty years, and it was the task of scientists to change fantasy into reality. Unfortunately, somewhere on the way he became a mad or bad scientist. I was worried that he was able to unleash dark forces. This was the reason I didn't want to sell the property, at least not until I investigated it myself, but I was too busy to fly to Scotland and also, in the end, I needed the money from the sale as I was about to get married. Then I stopped thinking about it till last week, when I read about the virus in Fife.'

'I think what you say sounds very interesting, but it's unlikely your theory is true, not least because nobody in our house got sick.'

'Really?'

'Really.'

'That is good to hear. Sorry to bother you. Still, if you find my uncle's diary, please send it to me. I will pay you for the postage.'

'I will. Goodnight.'

'Goodnight.'

When Andrew returned from work, late and slightly drunk, as was usually the case recently, Nicole asked him: 'Do you remember when you first felt unwell here?'

'To be honest, as soon as we came, even before we moved. I remember having a runny nose and headache, but then I didn't think about it. Why do you ask?'

'I wonder if this house was infected when Paul lived here.'

'Even if it was, no virus would survive so many years without people to feed on.'

'You said yourself that there were dust worms here and they suffocated you.'

'I was talking figuratively. Anyway, what does it matter? It's important that we are healthy and safe.'

'But people below us are dying.'

'It's their problem, not ours. As far as I'm concerned, given their hostility, they can all die.'

'Don't say that. We shouldn't wish death to anybody. Also, their problems might be our problem too, as a virus moves from one person to another.'

'After surviving these long months and regaining my health I won't be worried about any hypothetical illness. If anything, sickness and death of others might help me get promotion. Death also helps to preserve natural resources. Death is green.'

'You might not worry about it, but other people might worry on your behalf. Prepare yourself.'

*

Although the Scottish government kept repeating that the mysterious virus came from England, everybody was pointing the finger at Fife. One day Andrea knocked on Nicole's door and said: 'Do you know what is happening? There is a patrol on the Forth Bridge testing everybody who is travelling to Edinburgh by car. There is another one on Waverley and Haymarket for those coming by train. They look like aliens or cosmonauts, dressed in white suits, with their faces covered. They are building something two miles from here, in a wood. They covered the construction site with barbed wire, so nobody can see what happens there, but we think it is a lepers' colony. My neighbours say that they will take all of us there, to examine us, maybe even to dissect us, like rabbits, to check what we have inside. Of course, all of this will happen in secrecy, because the Scottish government would never admit that a plague started here and was passed to England.'

'It's impossible. They cannot do this to people. There is a law against conducting medical experiments against people's will. Besides, we seem to be all well here, on the headland. It's only people in the village who have these nasty symptoms and are dying.'

'Well, they say that we've released this poison on them out of revenge.'

'How we could do it without getting infected first?'

'They say that we got a vaccine; that's why our symptoms were so mild.'

'It's insane. Who exactly is saying this?'

'Everybody, but the leader of this conspiracy is an old guy named Douglas. His family lived in the village for many generations. He was a leader of the opposition against building of this estate and took Paul S. to court. Apparently, he also got his two bulldogs to attack Paul, although Paul never admitted this. As I'm saying this, shivers are going through my spine and I cannot forgive myself for buying the house here.'

'Stop it. There is no point in regretting it now. We need to ensure that nothing bad happens to us, either from people like Douglas or from the government. Shall we go and talk to him?'

'I'm not sure that's a good idea. The people down there really hate us. It's better not to challenge them.'

'But we are in this together. If they come for them, they'll also come for us.'

'You might be right, but I don't want to be involved with this crowd.'

'I don't mind doing it. After all, Andrew and I are successors of the man who started this conflict, even though we didn't know it, when we moved in here. I will see Douglas tomorrow.'

However, Nicole didn't have a chance to visit Douglas, as the following day he disappeared, together with his two dogs and some of the villagers. This caused panic among the people living on the estate, not least because Douglas almost never left the village and certainly not since the estate was built. Moreover, his departure looked like an escape, as he left at night, without telling anybody. Consequently, two days later, an unusual thing happened: the villagers called a meeting for both themselves and the inhabitants of the estate.

'I think we are all in a grave danger', said Martin, one of the villagers. 'All signs suggest the epidemic began here, either in the village or on the estate, and the government is closing-in on us. Already some of us have been summoned to go to the hospital in Edinburgh for check-ups. We've decided not to go and some of us, including Douglas Morrison, have left. We urge everybody who has received such an invitation to ignore it as, from the hospital, they'll move us to the gulag built nearby. This is the first thing: don't move, stay in Fife. But we need a longer-term plan.'

'I agree with you that we shouldn't respond to any invitation', said Nicole. 'But we cannot stay here indefinitely. We will run out of food, if not water.'

'Water is not a problem, a creek and a river run nearby. We can bring water from there in buckets.'

'But what about food?'

'In the first instance, we should make our own supplies: rice, pasta, flour, baked beans I can help with organising it. I even know the wholesaler in Dunfermline who will sell us these things at a reduced price. We can also grow our own food. In fact, I've done so for ages. I have my own courgettes, beans, parsnips, carrots. We can share our resources', continued Martin.

'It is all meaningless if they send police on us', said Andrea.

'If they do, we will defend ourselves. We have dogs and firearms. We can even dig out pitchforks from our sheds and cellars.'

Nicole giggled, as she found the idea of fighting the Scottish police with pitchforks comical, but she didn't say it.

'We need to create a special defence fund', said another villager. 'Who is in favour?'

It turned out that everybody was in favour, promising to chip 200 GBP per household. Nicole also agreed to pay, but not because she felt the need, but because she didn't want to attract attention. The meeting heartened Nicole, because the external threat of police or sanitary services were, for her, smaller than the threat from her neighbours living below. She decided to check the place where the camp was supposedly built in a nearby wood. She wasn't sure it was it, but there was a new clearing in the middle where there was some building material and machines for construction. However, they looked like something from the Lego set – the panels were in bright colours and the cranes were blue, red and yellow.

The trip to the meeting and the wood tired her, so she was happy to return home. She lay down on bed and closed her eyes. When she opened them, she noted that the walls around her changed from pale peachy colour to psychedelic purple, pink, green and yellow. She never saw colours of such intensity; it felt like triple coat of paint was put on each wall or rather the colours penetrated the walls.

'I must be dreaming', said Nicole to herself and fell asleep. She was woken up by a telephone. It was Andrew calling from work:

'What happened?', asked Nicole.

'I was promoted today.'

'That's great', replied Nicole.

'But this is not all. There are no trains back from Edinburgh to Fife tonight and the bridge is closed for the motorists. It seems as if you can leave Fife, but you cannot return. Somebody said this situation will last till the end of the week, while the public health people are running some tests. Given this, I've decided to stay with a friend. I hope it is okay with you.'

'Of course it is. Enjoy yourself', replied Nicole.

She didn't ask who Andrew's friend was; because she knew it was a woman, with whom her husband had an affair. But she didn't mind. In fact, it suited her, as it allowed her to explore the house on her own. They were, in fact, even, as each of them had found a new love since they moved to the headland house, except that her love was more elusive, less material and she felt superior this way. Nicole even felt disgust at the thought of having sex with a real, sweating, smelling, and snoring man, be it Andrew or anybody else.

*

Andrew did not return for the weekend and stopped phoning Nicole. Or, perhaps, she didn't hear his calls. She, on her part, stopped going to work and checking her work e-mail. She stopped checking her private e-mails as well, because she didn't know what was happening outside. She lowered the shutters on the windows, as she didn't want anybody to know that she was alone at home. Then she waited till the walls and ceilings grew colourful and soft. She knew she had to be patient because they didn't do this exercise for many years, so she delicately massaged them, as if they were patients who finally received treatment for a sprained back. Eventually a pink wall in her study gave in and she managed to put her hand inside it, as if it was soft tar. She did it just once, because when she tried again, the wall got hard again. This success, however, in penetrating the wall, put her in an excellent mood. The next couple of days she has spent moving inside and back and then resting in bed. She was so preoccupied with this activity that she forgot to eat and, although she was always slim, she lost much weight. She felt her ribs piercing her flesh and this made sleeping uncomfortable. Or maybe she was just sleeping too much. She got up and decided to visit the village shop. To her surprise, it was very well supplied, and even had fresh figs on this occasion, which she bought, together with courgettes, broccoli, leeks, carrots, green beans and potatoes. She decided to stew these vegetables as such a dish, which would be off-putting to Andrew who preferred steaks and pork chops, could last for days, maybe even for a week. She just needed to reheat it.

She praised the grocer for having such a variety of supplies, to which he responded: 'The wholesaler brought it all from Edinburgh and invited me to go there, to see what else he has on offer. He said the plague is officially over: there are no more patrols on the Forth Bridge, the trains are reinstated and people are required to return to their offices. However, I decided not to leave. I think it might be a trap. They want to lull us into believing that everything is normal, only to hunt us down, as if we were animals and take us to this slaughterhouse in the wood.'

'How do you know it is a slaughterhouse?', asked Nicole.

'Because it glows red and night and it stinks. I know the smell, as I used to work in an abattoir.'

'That's awful', said Nicole, but in reality she didn't pay much attention. She wasn't able to concentrate, because she couldn't see the grocer properly; his counters became fuzzy and he practically disappeared by the time she packed her shopping.

'I need new glasses', she thought. However, when she returned home, she saw everything clearly again.

She went to the kitchen and took vegetables from her bag with the intention of washing them and putting them in a pot, but wasn't able to do so because that colours in her house started to rotate, as if somebody invisible was moving from one room to another, only leaving traces of his presence behind. She felt compelled to follow this invisible creature, although she knew that in reality it was the house itself which was moving. She had awakened it, but the challenge was to make it open up. Progress was slow, or possibly she lacked patience, becoming angry when the house returned to its usual greyness and stiffness. Nicole left the vegetables in a sink and followed the trace, but without success. Eventually she fell asleep, without eating anything. But the following day she managed to fully cross the wall. Admittedly, it wasn't an easy or pleasant experience as she got stuck on the other side, unable to move. But at least she knew that there was something there, as she saw a road, but it was barricaded with pieces of strange material, like hard, yet sticky sponge. She lacked the strength to move them, even though they weren't heavy. It also required some effort to move back to her house because, in the meantime, the walls had grown stiffer again. When she found herself on what she now called the 'other side', she became very tired and had to return to bed. She didn't know how long she had slept, but she was woken by a postman, who brought her a registered letter. She had to sign for it and it took her several minutes to complete this task.

'Are you okay? Shall I call a doctor for you?', asked the postman.

'No. I was unwell recently due to this mysterious bug, but now I'm fine. I just need to eat something.'

She went to the kitchen to finally cook the stew, but was unable to put a large pot on the cooker. She had to distribute the vegetables among three pots and, in the fourth one, she put rice. 'This will be enough food for a week', she said to herself. Then she sat at the window, looking at the sea, waiting for her food to cook.

When the food was ready, Nicole mixed some of it in a bowl. Despite adding some butter, salt and pepper, it was tasteless, but she didn't mind. It even suited her that the food was so bland, as it balanced an oversensitivity in her other senses. She ate half a bowl and didn't bother to take it back to the kitchen. 'The last supper', she said sarcastically to herself, looking at the unappetising pulp. But she admired herself for making an effort to cook, when her mind was so far way from this kind of nutrition.

She remembered about the registered letter and decided to open it. She found in it a divorce petition from Andrew and decided to sign it, not because she agreed with his claim that their marriage broke down irrevocably, but because she didn't want to be pestered by Andrew again. Another letter she opened came from Andrew's solicitor regarding splitting and selling the house. It made her think that time was running out for her. If she wanted to move to the other side, she needed to hurry up. Paradoxically, this meant not to hasten, but be calm and patient. She sat in the middle of the bedroom and waited for the walls to start to talk to her. Gradually, the colours of the walls became warmer, as if moving from one end of a rainbow to the other. When they reached yellow, they started to soften and by the time they were in the middle of the way between yellow and orange, they had a consistence of tar on a hot day. When they became orange, they felt like a jelly which was about to melt into water. It was time to act. She moved inside the wall. For five minutes or so she was walking like colourful mud and felt the sticky substance enveloping her, like gigantic pieces of candy. Then she found herself in a tunnel. She walked through it, till she found a clearing, not very different from the one where the camp had been built previously. This time, however, there was no camp, but a large solid house at the edge of it. There was a handsome middle-aged man with grey hair standing in front of the house. She knew who he was and he knew her identity.

'Hello, Nicole, do you like my house?', he asked.

'Hello Paul. Yes, the house is perfect. Can I stay here?'

'Yes', he replied.

'How much is the rent?'

'Very little. I'm sure you will be able to afford it. This house is a bargain.'

He took her hand and they both entered it.

Permanent Residents

Ilona and Keith fell in love with this house at first sight. Truth be told, it didn't have the amenities Keith was looking for, namely an outside shed to put his bikes in and another one to store his machines for polishing and cutting stones, but these shortages paled into insignificance when they saw it. The most important of those was its fairy-tale quality, no doubt having something to do with the fact that it was very old. It was erected in 1739, as stated on its plaque, which also contained some initials, possibly of its first owner and a square of gold in the middle. After the partly ruined castle behind it, it was the oldest house in the village. It had three bedrooms on two floors, one for the couple, one for the guests and one which they could use as a study, a large lounge which until the 1970s served as a bookshop and a magnificent view of the sea from one side, and of the main street from the other. Moreover, the village of S., where this house adorned its high street, was picturesque and buzzing with life. The latter characteristic was in stark contrast to another place in Scotland where they used to rent a holiday apartment, which, although also located on the coast, had a lingering smell of neglect, even when they stayed indoors. The house was a bit expensive for them, but they decided that they could afford it, even if it meant making some sacrifices over the next few years.

However, Ilona and Keith did not want to show their enthusiasm too conspicuously, therefore they asked the owner some probing questions, such as 'Why do you want to sell it?' The woman, who was in her mid-thirties replied that this was because neither she nor her brother who inherited the house from their mother, ever lived there. She had been working and living abroad, recently in Morocco; her brother lived in a one-room apartment in Dundee and needed more money to buy something larger. This explanation satisfied Ilona and Keith and they put an offer on it the next day. It was immediately accepted.

Completing all the formalities took several months and then they were able to move in. It was great fun to go to charity shops and look on Gumtree for old furniture and rugs, in part because they couldn't afford new stuff for all the rooms and in part because they felt a house like this required old things, not necessary proper antiques, as they would be too expensive and might look pretentious, but things which already belonged to somebody else. After a week they bought all the necessary furnishings and decided not to hunt any more, as they exhausted themselves and wanted to spend the rest of their two weeks-holiday relaxing, enjoying their house and the village. It was indeed bustling with life. When they went for lunch to a café three houses from their abode, they were the last to get a table, and whilst eating they noticed some Japanese and Italian tourists. Ilona, who liked chatting to strangers, even asked them why they'd come to S. and they replied that they had it in their programme as the model 'Scottish village'. Ilona agreed mentioning S.' successes in the competition 'Scotland in Bloom' and being named the most beautiful small railway station in the country. The tourists were very impressed which added to Ilona's pride in having a house in S. She couldn't resist boasting that they had just bought the oldest house in the village.

Then they went for a walk through the park, full of multi-coloured l leaves and along the coast to the nearby village. They returned home in an excellent mood and to prolong it, Keith opened a bottle of wine. Just as he was pouring it into their glasses, there was a knock at the door. They gave each other a questioning look and then Keith went downstairs to open it, followed by Ilona. There were three people standing on the doorstep: two men and one woman, all in their fifties or sixties, judging by their faces and general demeanour. Ilona assumed that they were Jehovah witnesses, as they typically do their rounds in twos and threes, but they didn't have the humility on their faces, characteristic of followers of this religion.

'Good afternoon,' they said,

'Good afternoon,' replied Keith and Ilona. 'How can we help you?'

'We know you are the new owners of this house and we represent the residents of S. We try to meet every new resident, so that they feel that they belong to our community and we feel that they contribute to the village's wellbeing.'

'Nice to meet you,' said Keith.

'Nice to meet you too. Can we come in?'

'By all means, please do,' said Ilona. 'Would you like a cup of tea or a glass of wine?'

'A cup of tea will be nice.'

As Ilona went upstairs to put the kettle on, the visitors introduced themselves as Gordon, Alfred and Morag, and then Gordon asked Keith: 'Where are you from?'

'Me? I am from nearby, the village of B.'

'Are you really? But you don't sound Scottish,' replied Gordon, who came across as the leader of the group. Ilona thought that he might be an ex-policeman, as he had a judgmental look on his face and seemed to be used to telling others what to do.

'Well, my father didn't have a Scottish accent, and I went to a public school in Edinburgh, where I shed the little of the Scottish accent I gained at primary school.'

'What about you?' they turned to Ilona, who was just descending.

'I'm Polish, but I have been living in Britain for over twenty years.'

'Where?'

'All over the country: Banffshire, Devon, Yorkshire, Lancashire, wherever Keith was working.'

'I see,' said Gordon and then he turned to Keith again, clearly indicating that he regarded him as the head of the family: 'Are you now permanent residents of our village?'

'No, not yet,' replied Keith. 'We bought this house to use as a holiday place.'

'You see,' continued Gordon. 'We don't like residents who are not permanent. They aren't good for the cohesiveness of the community and for the local businesses. Bakers, butchers and fish-mongers will go out of business if people only use them in summer.'

Ilona was about to say that even if they were to live in S. permanently, the butcher, the fish-monger and the baker would have little business from them, because they were vegetarians and only ate dark, German-style bread, but Keith forestalled her by saying: 'We will keep coming more often than in summer, probably five-six times per year and when I retire, which is not far from now, I plan to move here semi-permanently.'

'Well, this is not good for us, as by the time you move here permanently, your neighbour the baker might go out of business,' added Alfred, who to Ilona looked like a little rodent, with sticking out teeth and a light-coloured, almost transparent moustache. Like a cartoon rat, he also smiled apologetically when saying unpleasant things.

'He might go out of business anyway,' said Ilona, 'given that these days most people do their shopping in supermarkets'.

'Not here. Here everybody shops locally.'

'How do you know?' asked Ilona. 'Are you checking people's receipts?'

'We don't do it personally, the local businesses do,' said Morag. 'They keep track of their customers and then we, the residents' committee, check how much each inhabitant spent per month locally. If this amount falls below a certain level, she or he has to make up for the deficit in cash.'

'What about the people on benefits or rough sleepers?' asked Keith.

'We don't have any of them here,' said Morag. She reminded Ilona of some older Polish women from the province, the type described as 'mohair berets': the pillars of Catholic conservatism. She even wore an equivalent of a mohair beret: a small dark-green hat, which she didn't take off during the visit.

'What is thus your solution to people like us? How much are we supposed to pay?' asked Ilona with a whiff of sarcasm, which, however, was ignored by everybody in the room except for Keith, who preferred if his wife remained polite, as the last thing they needed was to get into conflict with the people among whom they were meant to live.

'120 GBP per month'.

'Wow! That's a lot of money for us,' said Ilona. 'We stretched ourselves to buy this house and we had to pay so much extra because it is our second property: double the stamp duty and a second council tax. We really cannot afford to pay more simply because we want to have a holiday home. Can we opt out?'

'You can, but it is not worth doing. Those who opted out, don't live in S. any more.', said Alfred with his ratty smile. 'It is best to arrange the payment through a standing order. In this envelope you find the number of our account together with the report of how we, as a community of villagers, spend this extra cash. You will see there is value for your money.'

'We better go,' said Morag. 'Thanks for the tea. You have a lovely house. The most beautiful on this street and probably in the entire village. You were very lucky to get it.'

'Goodbye,' said the two remaining guests.

Once they left, Ilona kicked the door, through which they just passed.

'Fuck, fuck, fuck,' she shouted. 'I never thought that we'd find ourselves in such a situation. It was better not to buy this house. Maybe we should try to sell it straight away.'

'We cannot sell the house straight after we bought it. In this way we'd lose twenty thousand if not more,' replied Keith. 'Plus we like it here. The situation is temporary. Once we retire, we can live here, open a café or bookshop downstairs and take advantage of this fund, as it means that nobody goes bankrupt here, no matter how bad their business.'

'I don't want to open anything. I'd rather return to my country than to live among such horrible and greedy people. If they lived in Poland, they would try to tax the storks, because they only stay there for half a year,' replied Ilona.

'Be reasonable. Contrary to what we said, we can afford the extra hundred pounds. And they are right that people like us, who buy second houses, are destroying local communities.'

'Okay, do as you wish, but remember that I was against it.'

Keith poured himself a beer, as the wine suddenly tasted sour and then went to bed. Ilona followed him, as there was nothing which she wanted to do, plus she always followed Keith to bed, because she couldn't fall asleep when he was messing about at home. But she couldn't sleep, thinking how insincere, patronising and threatening the visitors had been. Poles are never like that – true, they are prepared to stab their enemies, but not with a smirk. Scots shouldn't be like that either, according to Keith. It was Albion which was meant to be perfidious, not Caledonia, but the three were worse than any English people she'd ever encountered. After a couple of hours Ilona got up, got dressed and went for a walk. It was shortly after midnight and in most houses the lights were switched off. After a while she realised that the remaining ones constituted a pattern – there was light in every sixth house, and she had a feeling that people were observing the street from behind the curtains. But when she looked at the window where there was a light it went out, as if the people in S. didn't want her to know that they took part in this night patrol. She had an urge to get a stone and threw it at one of the spying windows, but she didn't do it, knowing that if she did, she would have against her not only the local residents, but also the police. She caught a chill and returned home. She spent an hour or so sitting in the dining room and looking at the street from the window. It was the first time in her life that she'd had such a view, as before she always had a view of her own back garden or a private road. It occurred to her that such a position encourages spying and judging, so she closed the curtains and went to bed.

The next day was Sunday and they returned to their home in a village north of Preston and the following day they were back at work. Ilona had been planning to tell her colleagues about their new house, but in the end she didn't say anything as she didn't want to mention the visit of the residents' committee and it was now the only thing she could think about, when thinking about their house.

Keith also didn't want to talk to Ilona about the house, but she knew he kept thinking about it. The clearest sign of that was that when they sat down in the evening to watch their usual episode of a Netflix series, he wasn't drinking beer, only sparkling water. She knew that he did so to punish himself for being a weakling by not standing up to the visitors, , and to save money for the monthly ransom. However, the lack of alcohol made him irritable and he couldn't sleep at night. So after a week of this self-inflicted austerity Ilona bought him a crate of beer from his favourite micro-brewery and he drank two bottles while they were watching two episodes of 'Bloodline'. Afterwards they made love – the first time since they'd returned home from S.

In the morning Keith said: 'We will pay, but otherwise carry on as before, we won't allow the "permanent residents" to spoil our pleasure of not being permanent.'

Ilona smiled. She had a different view. As they showed in 'Bloodline', once you give into blackmail, you never stop, unless you are prepared to kill or be killed by your enemies. However, she didn't want to contradict Keith, not because she was submissive, but because it would make him miserable.

The weeks were passing quickly and Christmas was fast approaching. They decided months before that this year they wouldn't buy each other Christmas present because the house in S. was the greatest present they could give each other. Three weeks before Christmas Keith started to talk how nice it would be to go there and in the New Year see the fireworks in Edinburgh, which probably looked better from S. than from Edinburgh. They might go to the pub or drink mulled wine at home and stay in bed long into the morning. But ten days before Christmas, as she was walking to her office Ilona tripped on the icy pavement and broke her leg. The fracture was complicated and it was expected that Ilona would spend a lot of time in plaster.

Keith took two weeks of holiday to be with his wife, even though she didn't need so much attention. In fact, she preferred if Keith went to work, as she was in a lot of pain and wanted to deal with it on her own, but she didn't want to reject his offer. So they were staying at home, burning wood in an open fire, binge-watching Netflix series and drinking mulled wine, beer and champagne, sometimes all of them in one day, as the more alcohol was in the mixture, the easier it was for her to fall asleep. There was no more talk about saving in order to afford the extra expenses connected with their holiday house.

On Boxing Day, however, Keith decided to go to S., to check if their house was 'still in one place', as he put it. Ilona didn't go, because with her leg in plaster she wasn't fit for travel. She prepared for Keith a box with food, as she expected that the shops in S. would be empty by this point and, anyway, they wouldn't have the things they liked to eat over the Christmas period, such as dumplings with sourkraut and wild mushrooms and their own Christmas pudding.

Keith left early in the morning to avoid traffic. Luckily the roads were deserted and it took him a little over four hours to reach their house. As he was about to open the door, someone pulled on his sleeve. It was their neighbour, the baker:

'Hi. At last. We expected you and your wife to come for Christmas. Merry Christmas, if I can still say so.'

'Thanks. Merry Christmas to you too,' said Keith, eager to be on his own. 'We couldn't come as my wife broke her leg, so I came just for one night to check if the heating is still working and to bring some stuff from home.'

'Oh! I'm sorry to hear it. This is a pity as tomorrow we will have a village festival and an open meeting for all residents. You have to stay. We don't take "no" for an answer. I'm sure your wife will survive. She cannot be that horny,' he said and finished with a laugh.

This made Keith uneasy, but he joined in with a weak, fake laugh and said: 'Okay, I will stay an extra day.'

Then, when he was thinking that he was free, the baker said: 'Wait,' and he brought him a cardboard box with cakes.

'Thanks,' said Keith. 'How much do I owe you?' he asked.

'Nothing,' said the baker. 'This is a special Christmas present. It is a custom here that neighbours give each other presents for Christmas.'

'Oh, I didn't know that.'

'You will know the next time,' he said with this ratty smile, which according to Ilona, was a common characteristic amongst the inhabitants.

The house was very cold, but everything was there as they'd left it. Keith put the heating on and made himself a cup of tea. Then he phoned Ilona and told her that he decided to stay an extra day, to attend some village meeting, which might be an opportunity to renegotiate the deal with the 'village elders'.

'By no means, stay,' said Ilona. 'I will manage on my own or even begin catching up with work.'

Keith went to their bedroom and went to bed with a book, but couldn't concentrate. He returned to the kitchen, opened a bottle of beer and reheated the dumplings he made with Ilona before Christmas, while looking through the window. Despite the cold weather, there were a fair number of cyclists passing by. He also planned to bring their bikes here, but had no energy and motivation to pack them, as he didn't like to cycle on his own.

He'd looked out at this spot on the street on their previous visit, but then he had the feeling that he was observing those passing by – now he felt like that they were all looking at him. Instinctively he checked if his face or his jumper were dirty, but they looked okay.

The beer made him tired and he went to sleep. When he woke up, it was seven p.m. He decided to go to the pub, just to kill time, even though there were many jobs he could do in the house, such as unpacking boxes and measuring the walls to put up bookshelves.

The pub was quite full, but not excessively. Keith bought himself a drink, sat in the corner and started to watch the football on the TV. Usually though, he didn't like watching football or any sport, believing that this actually kept people from doing sports. After a while two guys joined him, and they started to talk. It turned out that one was from Edinburgh and the other from a nearby village. When he told them that he'd bought a house in S., they started to giggle.

'Didn't you know that this is the nastiest Scottish village this side of Edinburgh?' asked one of them, named Pete.

'I didn't know it, but I've started to realise,' replied Keith with an uneasy laugh.

'The prettier the place is on the outside, the uglier it is on the inside,' continued Pete. 'If you want to enjoy your holiday house, avoid places which have ever won competitions for the prettiest village or go straight to Majorca or Costa del Sol.'

'My wife and I don't like Spain. Besides, I'm from around here, so I wanted to return to my roots, when I retire.'

'Forget the roots,' said the other guy, Mark. 'People are not trees. They should be moving.'

'Now I see what you mean. Pity I didn't meet you some months earlier,' said Keith.

Back at home he couldn't sleep, most likely because he slept too much during the day. He wanted to talk to Ilona, but didn't want to disturb her sleep, knowing how difficult it was for het to fall asleep having her leg in plaster, so he ended up watching films on his mobile, which was something which he normally kept in contempt.

The next morning Keith took a train to Edinburgh, as being in the village made him depressed and he wanted to kill time before the evening meeting. He went to the Scottish Portrait Gallery, which he used to visit often when he was a teenager. Seeing the people from earlier epochs in their wigs and silly attire always had a soothing effect on him, although he didn't know why. Now he realised that this was because they represented time's power of erasure of both good and bad things. He needed to know that time will help him to deal with his problems, as he was afraid that he wouldn't be able to deal with them by himself. Age didn't make him stronger and wiser; it made him weaker and less self-assured, He felt tears filling his eyes and he had nothing to wipe them with so he went to the toilet. But after that he felt better and even went to the exhibition of Toulouse-Lautrec, which wasn't exactly jolly, but took him, again, to a different reality.

He had a meal in Edinburgh, phoned Ilona and when he returned to S., it was almost time to go to the residents' meeting. It was in a village hall, next to the church. When he arrived there, there were already quite a lot of people, maybe two hundred. Gordon, Alfred and Morag were there as well, talking to one man and one woman. Although there were so many people, they had immediately noticed Keith and gave him a sign to approach them. He did so and when he reached them, Gordon introduced Keith to the two people, who were also on the residents' committee and asked him to wait after the end of the meeting.

The meeting was about what the village had achieved in the last year and its plans for the next. There was much talk about the competition for the most beautiful village and small railway station. The station railway master was plucked from the crowd and for half an hour or so he listed what he did to get the award. He talked about his collaboration with the castle gardeners and setting up a small greenhouse behind the station from where some of the most beautiful flowers came to adorn the station. He also mentioned zero tolerance for drug and alcohol offences and vandalism. There were no vandals, drug addicts or drunkards seen anywhere near the station in the last decade, not least because photos of people who were last caught partaking in unsociable behaviour were still hanging in the display window in the village square. 'Naming and shaming is the best policy to keep our station beautiful,' he said to a round of hearty applause. Then there was a discussion about how to improve the results in the competition for the most beautiful village, in which S. slipped from being at the very top to being number 3. One reason mentioned by several people was the lack of flower pots in some houses as well as the poor state of some private buildings. The addresses of them were duly listed by Alfred. Luckily these buildings weren't in the centre of the village, but still the committee awarding the prizes had picked up on them. Gordon asked with his strong voice whether any people living under the said addresses were present at the meeting, but no one replied.

'We, the permanent residents, will deal with this problem,' he said with a twinkle in his eye.

There was also a shorter piece regarding the attendance of church services and various village ceremonies, such as the 'boat festival', the summer parade and the 'S.' carnival'. The following year the village would also have its first 'eco repair café' - the first in a place of this size, to cut down on waste and pollution. On the whole, the participation in the events was satisfactory, but there was an issue of some older people not attending due to poor health, as well the perennial problem of residents who were not permanent.

Morag then went on to present the committee's plan for preventing such people from buying properties in S. She summarised her meetings with the local estate agents, whom she tried to persuade not to advertise the properties nationally, only locally. Unfortunately, this suggestion was met with great resistance. Another proposal was to hold meetings with potential buyers before they made offers on properties. This already happened on couple of occasions, but then the estate agents prevented further meetings due to the fact that these buyers withdrew.

'In fact, they even wrote to the council to object on our practice on the grounds that it jeopardises their income and they threaten us with the court action,' finished Morag with indignation in her voice.

The thought that there was somebody in the region who had the strength to stand up to these people made Keith smile slightly. But it didn't improve his mood substantially. With every minute passing he felt worse and worse. He was sweating everywhere and his lips were dry. He wanted to drink something cold, ideally a can of beer straight from the fridge, but there was nothing like that on offer. Tea with milk, home-made scones and ham rolls ruled at such meetings.

At some point he became like the heroine from Hitchcock's 'Blackmail', who from the stream of dialogue was only able to discern one word 'knife'. For him it was just a different word - 'residents'.

Eventually the meeting was over and although Keith wanted to go home, he waited for the crowd to disperse to face his oppressors. He mustered the courage to be able to say that he wouldn't pay them more money, but they didn't mention money.

'I hope you enjoyed our humble parish meeting. As you could see and hear, we have great ambition for our little S.,' said Alfred with his ratty smile. 'We want it to be the most thriving and beautiful village in Scotland and by the same token, in the entire world, as it is now official that Scotland is the most beautiful country in the world.'

'I think it is a matter of personal taste,' said Keith.

'Well, here we believe this is an objective fact. But we didn't want to talk to you about our place in the hierarchies of beauty, but about something else,' said Gordon.

'What is it?' asked Keith.

'As you just heard, soon spring will come and we want all residents, and especially on this street, to have flowers in the windows and we understand that you and your wife might not be available to do it yourselves. Hence, we suggest that you give your spare key to us and we'll do it ourselves.'

For a moment Keith was thinking about telling them that he had no spare key on him, but he knew that it would only prolong the situation, as they would harass him by telephone and e-mail. So they walked together to his house and he gave them the key and then went to a Spar shop, to buy a couple of cans of beer. He asked the shopping assistant, a lad who couldn't be older than eighteen, if he knew who he was and whether he checks the identity of every customer, but the lad only shrugged his arms and looked at Keith as if he was mad, so Keith promptly paid and left.

At home he poured his beer into a glass and phoned Ilona to give her a report from the meeting, but didn't mention that he passed the key to the residents' committee. Instead he said that the meeting went well and there were no further attempts at extortion or assaults on their freedoms.

The next day he got up early to avoid traffic jams and because he yearned to be at home. All the way he was thinking whether he should tell Ilona that he gave the key to the residents' committee. He used to tell her everything, not because he had a special respect for truth, but because in this way he felt more secure: every problem was shared and halved when Ilona knew about it. He wondered why it wasn't the case anymore. Maybe he was worried that she would disagree with him or saw him as cowardly and defenseless. Probably she knew it anyway, as it's what he told her when they met, but it was a different thing to know in abstract and different to experience.

In the end he decided not to tell her and Ilona didn't ask. They practically didn't talk about the house throughout the remainder of their holiday and the following months. The only reference they did make to it when they talked about a robin which had started to visit their garden when Keith was in S. They called the little bird, whom they fed with seeds and dry fruit, 'our non-permanent resident'.

When the plaster was taken off from Ilona's leg, Keith and Ilona started to do more walking, discovering places in Lancashire which they never visited before and in March started to cycle, at weekends doing fifty-sixty miles a day. It was after one such trip that Keith told Ilona: 'I want to sell the house. I realised that this place is not for us. I'm so sorry I dragged you into it.'

'Are you sure?' asked Ilona.

'Yes, I am. It's not that I hate these "permanent residents"; it's just Scotland does not matter to me as it used to. I don't feel like I have my roots there; my roots must have moved and they are now in Lancashire.'

'Fine then. We have to approach the estate agent.'

'I will do it tomorrow.'

The estate agent was optimistic. He told them that houses like theirs sell quickly, because for folk from London they are still very cheap and if they weren't in a tremendous hurry, they could fetch a good price.

They replied that they weren't in a tremendous hurry and they could wait for somebody willing to pay them more than they paid themselves so that they wouldn't sell it at a loss. Over the next two months the agent showed it to six potential buyers. Eventually a family from London arrived whom Ilona and Keith met in person. They said that they wanted to buy it for their daughter who was about to start her studies in Edinburgh. For some reason, she didn't want to live in Edinburgh, though. The mother said:

'It is a lovely house, with so much character. When we saw it, we immediately thought that it would be a perfect place for her. And the village is so picturesque, with so many flowers. It is like heaven.'

'Yes, it is lovely,' said Ilona.

'May I ask you why you decided to sell it?' asked the father.

'We simply realised that it would be too expensive for us to keep two properties and we are not going to retire as early as we thought.'

'We understand,' said the couple.

Two days later the Londoners put in an offer, which Ilona and Keith accepted. In the end, they didn't lose any money. They even earned five thousand pounds, which they decided to spend on a trip to India.

The College Vampire

I was taken aback when I saw Mike for the first time. This was due to his pronounced ugliness and the incongruence of his entire appearance. He had blurry, discoloured and expressionless eyes, hiding deeply in sockets, surrounded not so much by wrinkles, as by layers of skin competing for the premium space under his eyes. His hair was thin, long and grey, reaching the tips of his long and equally thin and grey beard, his teeth were brown-yellow, matching the yellowness of his fingernails. He walked slightly bent and would look like a hermit, whom I remembered from Monty Python sketches, if not for the fact that his clothes were verging on the attire of a dandy. He wore a perfectly cut light-grey, almost white suit, which one sees rarely in England - especially along the corridors of a university - bright silk tie, a matching handkerchief in the breast pocket of his suit, and light-grey expensive shoes with narrow tips, whose content I tried not to imagine. The strangeness of his appearance was augmented by the ordinariness of his companion – a very short, middle-aged plump woman, called Betty, who was literally hiding in his elongated shadow.

They introduced themselves as lecturers in a department where I had started work two weeks earlier. They had been employed several months before me, hence more or less we were all new to this department. I greeted them politely, chastising myself for my antipathy to unattractive people. But soon it turned out that I was not the only one who found Mike odd and offputting. Other colleagues were also commenting on his fashion choice and his eccentricities and the bolder ones compared him to a vampire.

Outwardly, Mike and Betty were friendly with us, but they kept a certain distance. Equally, my colleagues didn't like being too closely involved with them. This was in part because their academic qualifications were unproven and their entrance to the university was unusual. Rather than going through the normal process of applying, being shortlisted and interviewed for the job, they appeared just like that; or at least this is what my friend Sophie told me. How it happened, nobody knew, as the head of department who employed them, retired and died soon after he brought them in. The gossip was that Betty used to work as a primary school teacher and Mike was a used-car dealer. Betty did not confirm it, but mentioned on a couple of occasion that Mike collected Jaguars, which forced him to rent an extra garage. He arrived at work in one of them.

When challenged about how they got their lectureship jobs, they claimed that they came by special invitation by the previous departmental head, to improve our courses and external engagement. With the passage of time, people who remembered their unusual entrance, left or retired and how they were appointed ceased to be an issue. In the meantime, Mike had progressed through the university ranks. He wasn't doing any research and little teaching, but was happy to fill any gaps in paperwork identified by people above him. He wouldspend weeks filling spreadsheets, checking whether spreadsheets filed by other employees aligned, signing forms when senior people were away and testing new administrative systems. His pet project, if one can say so, was dealing with complaints by staff and students. He was so good in dismissing them, that staff virtually stopped complaining about anything, knowing that, against Mike, there was no chance of their grudges being upheld.

As far as I remember, Mike was always at work, even on Good Friday and Christmas Eve. In fact, he preferred being at work on these days and became frustrated when a janitor threw him out from the premises at 3 pm, rather the usual 8 pm when the buildings closed. That said, Mike rarely arrived at work early; claiming that he liked staying late at night, going through his work when the buildings were quiet and absent of people, and, in the morning, he was too tired to get up and the rising sun hurt his eyes.

Over the years I learnt more about Mike's interests and habits, in part because it was difficult not to pick up on these things when one works with somebody and in part because I felt that Mike liked me. There was no chance for us to cross each other on the street without him stopping and asking about my health and workload, and making some comments about students and management. These comments were always abstract, as he was too cautious or detached to engage himself in gossip, maybe hoping that, in this way, colleagues would stay away from gossiping about him. Nevertheless, these chats allowed me to notice that his speech had an archaic inflection, not because he used archaic expressions, but because he tried somewhat too hard to talk in a 'modern way', be 'in the know', as if he was a grandfather trying to stay in tune with his grandkids, which essentially was the case. From these conversations I also learnt that he had a wife, Lisa, who retired many years previously on health grounds and rarely left home. Despite this, it appearedas if she never cooked, they did not engage in any shared pursuits and had no children. But Betty claimed that Lisa existed; she was just not well and, also, reclusive. Betty always confirmed that what Mike said about his private life was true. I even wondered if her role was to humanise Mike's extra-university life, of which he had little, being always on the university premises. Because he was so useful and committed to help those above him and, ultimately, competent, nobody asked what was there for him in attending seven-eight meetings in a row, constant hovering between different buildings and missing lunches, because he used the lunch breaks to attend more meetings. Surprisingly, when he attended working lunches, following assessment boards or periodic course reviews, he also ate little. He preferred to drink juices, smoothies, or red wine when it was available. When I asked him about it, he said that we are made of fluids and need only fluids to survive; solid food is for self-indulgence and it shortens human life. 'Look what sick people receive in hospital when they have a drip attached: it is usually blood or something which changes into blood quicky. People don't receive pieces of bread with ham through a drip.' Apparently, when he returned home from work, he prepared fruit juices for himself made from fresh fruit, mixed with iron and vitamins. This was all he needed to stay fit and heathy. Looking at him I wondered what fruit gave him such yellowy-brown 'smoker teeth' and nails, but I didn't ask.

Mike also specialised in 'acting roles', filling the gaps when somebody left, retired or was sacked. He went up the hierarchy to reach the position of 'acting dean', which he held for three years, till the new vice-chancellor began to employ new people to fill positions of power. Mike got demoted, but he wasn't made redundant, because the new dean quickly recognised his benefits and used him for all the paperwork he was too lazy or busy to do. Even by Mike's own admission, he wasn't a 'strategist'; his specialism was operations: making sure that the heavy machinery of the university was moving smoothy. However, he was successful in lobbying for the university buildings to stay open longer, so that students with poor accommodation or suffering from insomnia could find refuge on campus. In that endeavour, he was successful, as by the time I've left this university, all buildings stayed open till at least 10 pm.

When Mike was busy filling spreadsheets, people started to notice strange occurrences happening at the university. First, a couple of female students fainted, both in the evening, in a span of half an hour. This would not be unusual, were it not for the fact that neither of them ever had such an accident before and one claimed that she was pricked in her back before she lost consciousness. One of them also became anaemic afterwards and couldn't shake off this condition for the remainder of her studies.

These incidents of fainting and anaemia among female students grew more frequent and became the stuff of gossip. Often there were three-four faintings in a row, as if somebody was moving quickly between buildings to catch his victims and disappeared before getting caught. The university authorities decided to act, to prevent damage to the university's reputation which was already suffering due to poor retention rates and a low level of student satisfaction. It occurred to me that these markers of success had declined since Mike and Betty were employed, but I told myself that corelation is not causation. Moreover, no student complained about Mike orBetty specifically. They were both seen as competent, friendly and reliable. Extra work never tired Mike. He seemed to be unbeatable. There was thus a joke circulating about him; that when he started working at the university, he looked like he was 150 years old, but now he looked as if he was only 130, while in reality he was only 115. He heard this joke himself a couple of times and smiled mischievously, adding: 'You see, life is short, even when it is long, like mine. So make the most of it.' This, of course, garnered sympathy for him, because one needs to have both self-confidence and humour to brush off derogatory comments about one's appearance.

While Mike soldiered on, never losing his poise, over the years Betty aged considerably and it became more difficult for her to keep a façade of a cheerful, easy-going mummy. She gave impression of being constantly exasperated and small things led to her, barely concealed, outbursts of anger. I tried to stay away from her, but given that more and more people disliked her, she also gravitated towards me. When we met, we talked banalities, usually weather, food and Italy, as she was quarter-Italian and even had a house in Tuscany. When we stopped discussing these things, she asked me what people really thought about her and Mike. I kept replying that they were impressed by Mike's hard work and dedication to the university. However, rather than be glad about it, she grew even more impatient, as if suspecting me of hiding something. I, on my part, tried to find out more about Mike and their friendship. In this respect, Betty was evasive and her stories did not add up. Once she told me that they met through their spouses: Mike's wife and Betty's husband, who many years previously worked in the same consultancy firm. On another occasion, she informed me that she and Mike worked in the same college, which, however, in the meantime had closed down. On another occasion still, she just told me that 'it is a long story and not that interesting.' Knowing that I wouldn't try and squeeze out more information from her than she was prepared to share, I left my investigation at some point and limited myself to giving her a chance to talk to me whenever she wished to.

As Mike progressed up the university ladder, while Betty basically stayed in the same place, I saw less and less of them together. But when I saw them, they seemed not to be on such good terms as they once were. One time, by chance, I also overheard Betty telling Mike: 'You need to stop it. It will finish badly, if you continue', to which he responded: 'No, it won't. I know what I'm doing. You don't need to worry.'

Whether Betty was successful in convincing Mike to stop doing what he was doing, I was not sure, but the incidents of fainting began to feature in the local and national media, especially since two female students in two different incidents both claimed that they were attacked by a man with long hair and beard, who was uncannily similar to Bob from 'Twin Peaks'. This man put a damp cloth on their mouth, resulting in them losing consciousness. Admittedly, the first of these students was an obsessive fan of David Lynch's productions, so it was relatively easy to brush off her story as a sign of what would, in Victorian times, be described as 'a nervous disposition'; but when the second said the same thing had happened to her, it became more difficult to dismiss their claims. Again, both students seemed to lose much blood, but without any obvious signs of blood being pumped from them, such as the mark of a needle prick or a cut on the skin. But then needles used in blood transfusion have becomeso thin that they practically left no trace on the body.

I had noticed that, after every new incident, Mike's normally pallid face gained more colour, although he was not the only one who grew red in the face. Students got feverish that they might be the next victim of these strange attacks, whilst staff feared that it would affect our recruitment. It was bad enough working in a provincial university squeezed between two more prestigious institutions; working in a provincial university haunted by a nocturnal creature moved the situation from pathos to tragedy. And then, to make things even worse, a young student died on the premises. The official cause of her death was heart attack and the victim had a history of heart failure, but the fact that this happened in the evening, when she was on her own, made people liken this unfortunate incident to the faintings. Only a month or so after this tragedy Betty retired. She requested that no leaving party was organised, saying that she wanted to go quietly. Herrequest was granted. Nobody was concerned about her retirement as everybody was preoccupied with the 'vampire'.

The vice-chancellor, although he dismissed any link between the student's sudden death and criminality or unnatural forces having caused this death, felt compelled to act by introducing scanners to the buildings, preventing outsiders from entering. In the first year this led to many students and staff being unable to access their offices and teaching rooms, because the scanners often broke or they were unable to read the access cards correctly. Nevertheless, everybody assumed that it had become more difficult for outsiders to reach the premises. And yet, these accidents kept occurring and it was finally agreed that it was a man who was attacking young women, as a more robust medical examination showed that the assassin used some substance to put women to sleep and a very thin needle to extract blood from them and most likely a university employee. The next step was thus to install security cameras in each classroom. It was a costly operation, especially for my university, which had been haemorrhaging students for years. Consequently, in the next two years or so, it offered many of its staff early retirement or voluntary redundancy. During this period Mike and I both left, I to take a position at another university; Mike to retire. I lost track of him and indeed, of my old employer, because the majority of my former colleagues from the university had left before me. When, by chance, at conferences I met anybody working there, they told me that they had never heard about the 'college vampire' and neither did they know about Mike, suggesting that the university PR department was good in supressing such stories. After several years I had almost forgotten it myself, until one day, when walking to my office, somebody tapped me on my back. I turned and noticed that it was Mike. His hair had got even whiter than before, and his teeth darker. But, other than this, he had hardy changed. It turned out that he became a new dean and he was happy to see me, but not at all surprised. In fact, he told me that he wanted to work with me, when looking for jobs commensurate with his experience. 'You see, Betty died some years ago and I thought you would be her perfect replacement. You would be even better than Betty, as you are brighter.'

'Thank you', I said and rushed to my office.

Dream Factory

It was Paul's last full day in Edinburgh; the next day he was meant to fly back to New York. He felt that he could not take any more of these business trips, with meetings in high-rise buildings, the coded language used by the people there which made him feel on edge and the excessive amount of coffee and alcohol, which only gave him headache and made him sleepless. He thought he screwed it up too; the meetings didn't follow the scenarios he prepared and all four days he was in Edinburgh went excruciatingly slow. At times he even couldn't understand these Scots, whose soft, childish accents were like a cover-up for the most insincere plans. Everybody says that Scots are friendlier than the perfidious Albion, but he thought the opposite – for him they were outdoing the English in hypocrisy. He was also down because it would be more difficult than ever before to leave his job, as Sandra, his wife, who had so many ambitions for him, and so few for herself, recently became pregnant.

As the day was surprisingly hot for such as northern city, he decided to take a stroll through the centre. Apparently it was a day of a solar eclipse, but Paul doubted this could be observed in the middle of the city. Anyway, he never saw anything more unusual than the rainbow, as far as events in the sky were concerned. He left his mobile at the hotel, so nobody could get hold of him – neither his boss, nor his colleagues from work, nor his wife. At first he walked around the castle, admiring the magnificent building, perhaps the best-situated castle he knew of and then took a steep narrow back street. The beauty of Edinburgh's centre was that it consisted of such steep narrow streets, in which one could easily get lost but also miraculously emerge in front of the familiar building. The important thing was not to think too much about one's destination, just let the streets lead you, as somebody told Paul the previous day. He followed this advice, especially as he had no specific plan, except to strengthen his legs, sit down in a café, drink a soda, take another aspirin and read a real paper. Unfortunately, his headache got worse, and he felt like his lips were getting dry, but there was no cafe or even a shop to buy a drink. Suddenly he found himself in front of a building with a neon sign saying 'Dream Factory.' The building looked like an old cinema, although as far as he knew, there were no more cinemas of this sort left in Britain. He went in, as he expected it to be cool inside and he thought that perhaps they sold soft drinks there.

Inside there was a dark corridor lit with a very weak, red light. He had to walk for some time until he reached a small desk, where a Japanese-looking receptionist greeted him in English with a strong Scottish accent:

'Do you have an appointment, Sir?'

'Yes,' he said.

'What is your name?'

'Paul Taylor.'

'I do not have you on my register, but this might have to do with the power cut we suffered yesterday, which wiped some information from our system. Is this your first visit?'

'Yes.'

'So you need to see our personal dream advisor first.'

They carried on walking this long corridor which was even more badly lit than the reception area. The uneven walls were painted in dark red and there were many doors, as if it was a hotel full of small blind rooms, which are not uncommon in cheap hotels in China and Thailand. Paul was taken to one such room, indeed lacking windows. The only furniture there was a small desk with an old-style PC and two chairs. On one of them sat an old man, also looking distinctly Asian and he had the same Scottish accent as the receptionist. He introduced himself as 'John' and said:

'Welcome to Dream Factory. Our motto is "We dream for you." Our philosophy is based on the premise that dreaming is a hard and dangerous work. Dreams can make you exhausted and unhappy, even more so than insomnia. Therefore we want to ensure that your sleep will be restful and satisfactory and help you survive your daily life.'

'How does it work?'

'First we try to establish what type of dream you want and what characters you want to insert into it. Then we take a scan of your brain to extract the appropriate mental images to place in what we call the master narrative. Usually these will be people you want to see when sleeping: your beloved or, conversely, your enemies. Once the right combination is achieved, you have a dream trial. If you are satisfied with it (and most customers are), we work with you on your long-time "dream plan," where you decide how much of your sleeping time you want to devote to quality time and how much to leave to unstructured sleep.'

'How do you insert these dreams?'

'We inject them with a special syringe; as this ensures that they work almost immediately. However, it is also possible to take them in the form of a pill.'

'How is it better than taking LSD or something like that?' asked Paul.

'Many people ask us this question. To begin with, drugs are poison; everybody agrees on that, even their users and manufacturers. Sooner or later they will kill you. By contrast, our dreams are completely safe. We represent biocybernetics, not some junkie business and we have almost a hundred years of experience. Our headquarters are in Vienna, not in Columbia or Mexico. This is our founding father – he pointed to a portrait of an oldish, baldish man with a beard and a cigar, which was vaguely familiar, but Paul could not recollect where he'd seen it before.

Secondly, people take drugs to cope with their daily reality, even if the drugs affect their sleeping pattern. Our injections and pills work only when our customers are asleep. Hence they are entirely private. There is no danger that you will embarrass yourself by acting erratically or aggressively as is the case with users of heroin, LSD or meth.'

'Are they addictive?'

'Not in the usual sense of the word. It is you who decides what to do with the dreams. You can request new narratives or develop them with our designers or on your own. It is like moving from a primary school, through secondary, up to university. First you need a teacher who does everything for you, then one who assists you and finally you can do it all by yourself.'

'How much does it cost?'

'This depends on the type of meta-dream you choose. We have three basic types: the loving type, the killing type, the avant-garde type. The loving type is the cheapest – it is around 150 GBP per dream. Next is the avant-garde type – about 200 GBP per dream. The killing type is the most expensive – 250 GBP per dream. You can reduce this cost by up to 30% by agreeing for us to insert an advert into your dream, like popular songs on YouTube. The only difference is that you cannot skip the advert. You have to dream them to the very end. But they are, of course, short. We also try to make them fit the actual dream. Our team designs the adverts in the same way we design dreams. The dream trial costs 100 GBP, irrespective of the type of dream and lasts about two hours.'

'What are these types?'

'The loving type is, in a nutshell, the dream of having sex with a person you wish or more than one, for that matter. In the killing type you torture or kill people you hate. In the avant-garde dream you do not see people, only soothing images and hear pleasant sounds. We try to customise them too'.

'Can you kill real people in these dreams – people I know?'

'Yes, that is the beauty of it. You can place in your dream real people and do with them what you want. There can be historical people too and imaginary, as long as they are clearly defined. You can kill Hitler, if you wish, and sleep with Angelina Jolie.'

'What do people usually choose?'

'Few people opt for Hitler. Most people want to kill those they know and sleep with those whom they do not know.'

'Like who?'

'This year among heterosexual men the most popular are the Taylors: Taylor Swift and Taylor Schilling. Among those who are dead the leading ones are Marilyn Monroe and Princess Diana. But there are also national variations.'

'Can I have a threesome with Monroe and Diana?'

'Yes, but it will cost you an extra 50 GBP. 200 GBP in total.'

'This will be more expensive than a night with a hooker.'

The man smiled, and then answered:

'A customised dream is a very complex commodity and still a very new one. Imagine yourself being the first customer who bought a laptop or a mobile phone. Things like that weren't cheap when they first entered the market.'

'Are there any cheaper companies doing this?

'Yes, they are, but they are not reliable. If you go there, it will be like buying crack cocaine from an unknown dealer.'

'Can I also commit suicide in my dream?'

'Yes, though such dreams are a bit dangerous. It might be difficult to wake up from them.'

'OK. I know what I want. First I want to kill the annoying man whom I met in Edinburgh and… '

'You do not need to tell us all that', John raised his hand to stop Paul. 'Just put this headgear (you see it is very light and comfy, not like these cosmic helmets from old science fiction films) and imagine the people you want to place in your dreams. First in the killing dream, then the loving dream. Press this button after you finish with one type of dream.'

Paul put the headgear, which indeed felt very light and soft, like a bandage. He wasn't certain if he closed his eyes or not, but for sure he found himself in a new place: a kind of huge curiosity shop, dark and musty, and filled with various things from his past, mostly those which he disposed of. There was a Santa Claus costume which he was asked to wear when he was a child, many old toys, a pile of CDs Sandra threw away when they moved to a new apartment and even a piece of a fancy cake he failed to eat because Sandra was unwell and they had to leave a party. These things were arranged in no particular order, as in a junk shop. When he was approaching them, he noticed that behind them there was somebody a person, who gave him this thing or took it away from him. The things were much larger than the people, as if it was a warehouse serviced by gnomes and they had shy smiles on their faces, as if they were asking for mercy. After all, it was meant to be a killing dream. But Paul had no time to stop and talk to these people or inspect the old treasures – something forced him to hurry up. The further he went, the less crowded became the warehouse and the more light was filling its space. Eventually he reached its end, where there was a large, old-fashioned wooden gate. Unfortunately, it was locked, and there was no way to open it. He was kicking the door, but this only made his body ache. Suddenly he noticed that there was a small eye-shaped object on the frame, like a small knob or a large button. He pulled it and the door started to move with a crackle. When it happened, Paul started to regret that he didn't stay a bit longer and didn't eat the cake, which looked delicious. But there was no way back – he was now pushed forward, leaving the junk behind. Eventually he heard somebody saying, 'He is waking up.'

He opened his eyes and saw a man in a white uniform.

'Is this a dream factory?' he asked.

'You could say so,' the man said with a smile. 'But we are slightly more versatile. We also try to wake up those who are sleeping. You are in a hospital.'

'What happened to me?'

'You lost consciousness. Most likely it was a reaction to a solar eclipse. You were lucky a Japanese tourist called an ambulance.'

'How long have I been here?'

'About two hours. It doesn't feel very long, but we were worried about you. It looked like every part of your body was switching itself off, as if preparing to take you to a different reality. Very unusual', continued the doctor.

The doctor asked him to stay in the hospital for another day, but Paul insisting on leaving, as he had a plane to catch.

Back at the hotel, he checked his mobile. Sandra was texting him to phone her back. When he phoned her, she told him that she had to rush to a hospital, as there was a danger of a miscarriage and how angry she was, not being able to contact him at this time of anguish. In the end everything was fine and the baby was saved. She talked about all these things in her typical minute detail, managing to squeeze in every sentence a drop of self- pity and accusation.'

Finally she said, 'and what about you?'

'Me, as usual. The meetings were stressful and I had a bit of a sleeping problem. But it is all over now.'

'Of course, with you always everything is fine, therefore you don't understand how it is for me to be here on my own, with all these worries, when you are enjoying himself.'

Paul started to feel again very tired and uncomfortable. It was in part because his clothes were hurting him, especially his tight trousers. He put his hand in his pocket and took out from it a small eye-shaped object, like a little knob. He started to squeeze it and felt like he was about to fall asleep.

The Mute Lady

Two years ago we bought a holiday house in Aberdour, a village on the East coast of Scotland. Our house was the second nearest to the railway station and the Aberdour castle (which according to a local leaflet, was one of the two oldest castles in Scotland), and the first house which was occupied, at least from time to time. We never saw the next-door neighbours to our right and on our left was a bakery. One day I told Alex jokingly that if somebody was running away from the castle or the station looking for help, we would be the first who they'd approach. This is exactly what happened, albeit not in reality, but in my dream which I had one of these wintery nights between Christmas and New Year, which I spent with Alex in Aberdour, while my husband was travelling for work in England.

It was also a wintery night in my dream. In it I was about to go to bed when I heard knocking on our door. When I opened it, I saw a woman of an undefined age. She looked strange, because she was dressed only in a long creamy-coloured dress and had wooden clogs on her bare feet, and long blond shiny hair which were moving even though there was no wind. She was very pale and she didn't say a word, only pointed to her mouth, so I guessed she was hungry. I sat her at the kitchen table and prepared for her some sandwiches and a cup of tea with milk, to which she nodded approvingly and put her hand on her heart, to show her gratitude. When she was eating, I noticed that not only she was pale, but her body was practically transparent - I could see bones under her skin. Moreover, she was eating in an unusual way, as she didn't bite from the slice of bread, but tore out a piece and put it in her mouth, as I saw on some films, showing the life of Russian peasants in pre-Revolutionary times. Yet, although she ate this way and was thin, pale and haggard, she didn't look like a peasant. On the contrary, there was something regal about her, as if she was used to giving orders.

When she finished, she asked me for a pen and a piece of paper, on which she drew Aberdour castle, but not as it looked now, mostly in ruins, but when it was in its full glory in the medieval times. The castle on her picture had a cellar where there was a dungeon and she drew there a woman with long hair and two children, a boy and a girl. I guessed the woman was herself and the kids were her offspring. She also drew a king or possibly an earl, given that the castle was not a royal castle, but only the home of some Scottish aristocrats. There was a woman next to him and then she put a crown on the head of the mother and crossed it and then drew it on the head of the woman standing next to the king. I thus gathered that she was a queen or a princess abandoned by her husband for another woman and that her (ex)husband imprisoned her. The story seemed very medieval to me, which made sense, given her look and the way she acted.

I made a sad face when she finished, to express my sympathy. There was no point to tell her anything, as she was obviously deaf and I didn't want to wake up Alex whose bedroom was next to the kitchen. She put her hand on her heart again to thank me, but also took my hand and moved my finger from her kids and herself to the place occupied by the king and the new queen. I realised that she wanted me to help her overcome her predicament. I sighed as helping people was something which used to tire me immensely in my middle age. I took another piece of paper and with much less skill than her drew a railway station and the train, and Alex and myself, and like her, put a finger on us to move us to the train, to show her that we were about to leave. She asked when and I replied the day after tomorrow. It was a lie, as we were meant to spend four more days in Aberdour, and also a mistake – I should have told her that we would be leaving the same day. This is because one day in a dream lasts much longer than one day in reality - one can build a fortress during a dream of this length. Not surprisingly, the Mute Lady was happy and made a sign which I interpreted as 'plenty of time'. In this case it was plenty of time to take her to a better place from which she could fight back for her lawful inheritance. She was happy to inscribe my entire family into this plan, even though I told her that we were rather apolitical and my husband was not particularly welcoming to strangers.

Then she ordered me to make more sandwiches and go with her, and she took me to the castle and stopped near the cellar-cum-dungeon. There was nothing inside – an empty hole, like a socket without an eye. There was some wood, tools and rubbish scattered around it, a sign of on-going excavation and restoration of the castle. But this is not how the Mute Lady saw it. She descended into the cellar twice and climbed back, each time with an invisible child, as suggested by the position of her arm and the fact that she was kissing the air where the head of the child was meant to be. Then she took me to the dovecote, which served her as a storage area – she kept her some kitchen utensils, clothes and trunk with golden coins and other valuables. It occurred to me that it would be more practical to live in a dovecote and keep things in a cellar, but there was no time to ask such questions.

I realised that she entrusted me with the mission of saving her entire family and punishing the unfaithful earl. I thought that it was a relief that all these royalties were phantoms; otherwise I could end up in this dungeon myself for supporting the wrong branch of the royal family and even be tortured. At the same time I knew that they were phantoms only in this layer of reality; if I fell asleep, they became visible and tangible. This was because the deeper I fall asleep, the more dead people I encountered and the more I lost from those who were real to me in the world of my consciousness. On this occasion I dreaded that I would lose Alex, who would be trapped in this layer of reality between the material world and a dream within a dream. Hence, I couldn't fall asleep. Luckily there was plenty of coffee in the kitchen.

The Mute Lady left me at the entrance to the dungeon and told me that she would return the next day with her kids and their belongings. Before she left I asked her to give me her name and she said 'Johanna' or 'Joanna'. She didn't ask about mine, which I attributed to her regal ways – the royals do not have time to learn their subjects' names. By the time we parted, I was proficient in sign language – the advantage of dreaming in both senses (sleeping and wishing for something) is that one learns things much faster than in reality. It also occurred to me that it was a blessing that we used drawings and sign language to communicate, because if she spoke in Middle English, most likely I wouldn't understand her.

I returned home and made myself a large pot of coffee in order not to fall asleep till I wake up from this dream. But after a couple of hours I gave into tiredness and went to bed. Luckily, when I wake up, I was still in the same dream as before and Alex was sleeping in his bed, next door to the kitchen. I decided to go out to do some shopping, as after Johanna's visit we were low on bread, cheese and other essentials. While out, I noticed a small gathering in front of the railway station. I went closer to find out what it was about and it turned out that it concerned the renovation of the castle. Two older women, one short, one tall, with loud speakers, were leading a meeting and they said that the renovation was dragging on, especially given that the castle was not exactly the Notre Dame.

'The work ethic of the labourers leaves a lot to be desired, there is no proper signage and the tourists don't know which part of the castle they are allowed to visit and which is off-limits. Somebody made a hole in the wall and some tourists have taken advantage of that, visiting the castle without buying tickets. Most importantly, the cellar is a safety hazard – a visitor can easily slip and break a limb,' complained the taller of the two women.

'The castle garden looks more like an abandoned picnic than a historical monument,' continued the shorter one. 'Also, it looks like some homeless people or, worse, hippies, started to occupy the dovecote and the cellar, as at night the residents from the neighbouring houses hear moaning and crying coming from these places. Council workers have also found pieces of cloth,covered in faeces and blood and even soiled nappies made of some strange material, like wool. There's also been knocking on some doors at night, but when people opened the door, there was nobody there. We must ensure that the work on the castle is completed in a timely manner and that the intruders are banished from our community.'

'For this purpose, we've set up a committee, demanding that Historic Scotland patch up the hole in the wall surrounding the castle, lock the door to the dovecote and cover up the cellar, so that nobody can get in there. We prepared a petition which we would like each adult inhabitant of Aberdour to sign,' concluded the tall woman, before approaching the people surrounding them with a piece of paper. Soon she gave it to me to sign.

'What exactly do you want to be done with the cellar?' I asked her.

'To fill it with concrete, as it was before. If the people who are in charge don't do it, we'll do it ourselves. Do you have anything against it?' she asked me, clearly unhappy that I expected her to repeat such information.

'No, of course not,' I said, signing and thinking that I have to warn Johanna about these plans.

'Thank you,' said the petition-holder, moving to my neighbour when the other woman announced: 'Our petition will also be available online. Make sure your neighbours sign it, if they haven't done so already.'

Back at home Alex was already awake and asked me what the people were doing practically in front of our house. I explained to him that it was to do with the noise and disruption during the castle's renovation. I was on the verge of telling him about Johanna whom I promised to take with us to our home in Lancashire, but something prevented me, most likely the concern that he wouldn't believe me. So I didn't say anything.

A couple of hours later Alex discovered that his iPad stopped working that night and started to nag me to return home, where we had a spare one. To his surprise, I agreed. We packed our stuff and decided to take an early afternoon train to Edinburgh. When we were on our way to the station, I noticed some activity by the castle. I left Alex with our suitcases to check what was going on there and noticed that the workers had put metal bars on the entrance to the cellar. There was some noise coming from below.

'Somebody is crying in there,' I said to the workmen.

'Nobody's there; it's an echo,' replied one of them. 'The cellar has been built in a way which attracts the smallest noise and amplifies it. This is the reason the cellar was filled in, when it stopped being used as a dungeon. This is what this whole protest is about – the echo.'

'I see,' I said and left in order not to miss the train.

Before we boarded the train, I woke up – it was the postman who woke me up or so I thought, as somebody put something through the letterbox. I went down and found an invitation to a lecture by some historian from Edinburgh titled 'The Mute Lady of Aberdour: Facts and Myths'. I opened the door to see who'd brought it, but there was nobody there.

The Sorry Tellers

Emma joined the 'Real Thoughts' support group reluctantly, as she disliked organisations. It was a marker of her despair that she put her distaste aside, paid the registration fee and turned up at the meeting at the centre of Manchester. The first impression was disappointing, as the hundred plus group turned out to be dominated by noisy simpletons with the history of religious evangelism; the type one associates more with the American South than the English North, but obviously nutters are everywhere. However, there was also a minority of those who, like Emma, gave impression of being sane and embarrassed to find themselves in such a company. They gravitated towards each other and decided to meet again in a smaller circle. During the second meeting one of them, Robert, proposed to call them 'The Sorry Tellers', in contrast to 'The Happy Tellers', who kept talking about love of God which not only placed on them special obligations, but made them extra happy. The Sorry Tellers consisted of two computer programmers, one psychiatrist, one university lecturer, one writer and one fashion model. One of the computer programmers left after the second meeting, admitting that he was looking for something different. Because the group became so small, John, the psychiatrist, who facilitated organisation of the Sorry Tellers, proposed to meet in their houses, rather than specially rented venues. Each meeting focused on one person, who shared his or her story with the rest of the group. Emma was entrusted with taking notes from the meetings. What follows are extracts from these notes.

A Man with the Past

When time came for Robert to introduce himself, he said that he is a 'man with the past'. The past always hold him back; it was his negative capital and it was not even his own past, but his father's. Robert's father came from a rich and successful Scottish family. He had four brothers and one sister. However, due to unfortunate circumstances, such as a premature death of his first child (Robert's older sister), and Robert's mother, who died in a car crash, he lost most of what he had: his job, social position and support of his siblings, who subtly, yet effectively, ostracised him. He had difficulty to cling to a job, occasionally was unemployed and took early retirement. Money was always a problem in his home. Robert's dad also battled with depression and seeing his father crying or just looking through the kitchen window, to avoid showing his sad face to his son, was breaking Robert's heart. The worst time for them was Christmas, when they shared humble meals, prepared pretty much the same way as their normal meals, and knowing that the rest of their family was spending their time together, attending lavish parties and handing each other expensive gifts.

Given the circumstances, Robert did quite well in life, going to the university and getting a scholarship to do a PhD in physics. After that he got a university position. On his own account, he was good in his job, but dealing with the past took so much energy that he could not devote himself to building his future. He missed opportunities for promotion and because he had to look after his father, he could not even try to move abroad, where his chances were better. He never married nor had a long-term relationship, despite being quite good looking (as Emma could confirm) as falling in love was too much of a luxury for him. Needless to add, he had no children, while his cousins had in total eleven children and several grandchildren. This added to his inferiority complex, as it further undermined his place in their clan and made him feel as if he was going through life with a different speed than the rest of his family. His future transformed into the past before he was able to grasp it. Paradoxically, it was even more the case after his father's death. Predictably, his father died of heart failure.

This sombre occasion was an opportunity for the family reunion; they could ignore Robert's father when he was alive, but it was more difficult in the hour of his death. All his siblings attended Robert father's funeral and only one of his nephews did not come, ironically the only one who was in regular contact with them; this was because he lived in Australia. Robert noticed that his uncles and aunts were still in good health, despite being now in their seventies or eighties. The same was also true about his cousins and their children. And yet, he sensed decline. It felt like they merely fed on what they received from their ancestors without adding much to their heritage. They performed the same jobs as their parents, being lawyers, doctors, politicians, economists, yet without reaching their elevated social positions. For example, his cousin Rosie was a mousy GP, who seemed to have no ambition beyond providing for her family, while her father, uncle Richard, who was labelled the greatest surgeon in the whole empire, was a formidable figure. Even now, in his eighties, he was switching with ease from medicine to physics and convincingly argued why Hawking was a minor figure in comparison with Heisenberg. Robert also noted with anger, but also certain admiration, that the sombre occasion did not prevent Richard from criticising his brother for marrying beneath him and engaging in minor causes rather than trying to reach the top of his profession.

Already in the church, instead of thinking about his father, Robert started to reorganise in his mind his relatives' past. He imagined that his cousin Philip learnt that the man whom he treated as his father, uncle Andrew, was not really his father, because his mother had an affair with Richard. Uncle Bruce, the financial director of one of the largest British firms, who made fun of Robert's father's financial inaptitude, turned out to be a fraud, embezzling millions of pounds. Robert even slightly smiled when thinking about these twists. Ironically, the family interpreted his drama-free demeanour as a sign of his strength in the face of great loss; hence a sign that he belonged to their clan. Of course, he did not deny it.

Several months later what John imagined started to materialise. Mark, who looked fragile at the funeral, had died and his daughter Virginia, upon clearing his father's archive, discovered some letters he wrote to his lover, who turned out to be his sister in law. Robert learnt from the same Virginia that Bruce's affairs were investigated for some years by various state offices. But the best scoop came when a nosy journalist published an article alleging that uncle Jim, a retired politician, sitting in the House of Lords, and a media celebrity, was in fact a paedophile. Even in his late seventies Jim retained his taste for young flesh and was driven in limousines to orphanages where he 'bonded' with boys as young as five in exchange for financial gratification for their guardians.

(Emma added in the footnote that the whole group sighed with a mixture of admiration and indignation to learn that Robert was the famous 'Lord Jim''s nephew and possibly a person responsible for revealing the truth about this man, whose paedophile exploits were filling front pages of the national newspapers not a long time ago.)

There were more revelations of this kind, although not of the same gravity as the story of 'Lord Jim'. Like an updated version of Louis from the Ealing comedy *Kind Hearts and Coronets* (a favourite movie of Robert's father), who every day was checking newspapers to find who died and who was born into D'Ascoyne family, Robert was browsing the internet to find out what new misfortune befell his relatives. Within a year Robert's family, previously so united, was torn apart. One by-product of these circumstances was his cousins' new sympathy towards Robert. They also finally acknowledged that they had no moral grounds to distance themselves from his father. The new situation, however, did not bring Robert moral satisfaction and even less a sense of closure. He now felt more trapped in the past than before and came to conclusion that he was a meaner person than his uncles and cousins, who were merely selfish and pompous, rather than harmful. This realisation brought him to 'Real Thoughts'.

A Killer

Emma started writing 'fiction' in her early thirties. Once she started, she could not stop. She was the ultimate realist, writing only about people and situations she knew first hand. This explains the fact that for some years she did not do anything with her short stories except from showing them to her small circle of friends. Whenever she did so, however, she was careful not to send her story to people who might know her characters. This was because, like every writer, she tried to add drama to her stories, not unfrequently by killing her protagonists. Death is regarded as the most clichéd element of literature, but Emma believed that in books we encounter not too many deaths, but too few. Next to birth, death is the most *real* element of one's life. We cannot guarantee that somebody will fall in love, but we can be sure that this person will die. This also means that death provides more narrative opportunities than other events. Emma also believed that death is not accidental; there is a fit between the way people live and the way they die. Therefore she was starting her stories with death and then was 'writing back', trying to establish what kind of beginning led to such an ending.

Naturally, it is sad to kill people whom one loves, so Emma excluded them from her 'fiction'. Her first story was about her previous boss who harassed her sexually. He used to come to her office, put his bear-like paw on her hand, and kept talking to her for up to two hours at the time, bringing his large torso closer and closer to her. To add insult to injury, he regarded his interest in her as some kind of favour, because Emma was single, while he was happily married or so he said. The worst thing about this 'affair' was that when he eventually moved to another company and disappeared from her life, she started to romanticise him. In her mind he changed from a fat, sweating bastard, to a presentable man, whom she rejected because of her old-fashioned morals. She loathed herself for that. But it required time and effort to make her mental image of him resemble reality. Writing accelerated this process. In Emma's novella, she made him suffer from high blood pressure and strokes, described with cruel precision. No need to add that the last of these strokes turned out to be deadly.

Another piece she wrote was about some people who lived in a terrace next to her house. When they moved in, they seemed like a nice, childless couple, but with the passage of time Emma's relations with them deteriorated. This was largely to do with the noise they produced. At weekend they left the house in the hands of workers who made renovations. From Saturday morning till Sunday evening Emma's space was invaded by the drilling sounds and sometimes already on Friday evening she was hearing the drilling, although perhaps it was only in her head. When she complained about it to the culprits, they advised her to leave her house for weekends and see some friends, as 'all single people of her age do.' She hated them for patronising her and yet she had no strength to talk them back. She was just waiting for them to finish making up their bloody house. Unfortunately, when the renovation was over, they started to produce babies. The first one was born only two or three weeks after the end of drilling and most likely Emma missed one of her two 'free' weekends because indeed she used one of them to visit her friends. By the time Emma left this house, they had three children and the fourth was on her way. The babies proved even worse than the construction workers, because the workers struck only at weekends while the babies were making noise all year round, perhaps because their parents paid little attention to them. The worst was the oldest. He was constantly yelling and bullied the other kids. It felt like his ultimate goal was to wreak havoc wherever he appeared. Emma gathered that his bedroom was neighbouring her bedroom, with only a thin wall dividing them, as at night somebody amused himself by kicking and scratching his side of the wall and the other kids were probably too small to do it. She was thinking that her life was now like a cross between *The Shining* and *The Omen*. Emma tried to bring this noise to the attention to the child's parents, but they reacted aggressively. They stopped saying her 'hello' and when they had guests, they pointed to them her window and made gestures suggesting that Emma is not sound on her mind. The boy in Emma's story fell when climbing the fence dividing the properties of his parents and the neighbours and damaged his brain. He was bed-ridden for many months, before dying. The short story was her literary breakthrough –

she got the main award in an important competition. The judges praised Emma for her eye for detail (she described the injury and death of the boy with clinical precision thanks to taking voluntary work in children's hospitals and hospices) and compared her work to South American magic realism, although when she started her writing, she was not familiar with this literary current.

Emma did not need to finish her story. The Sorry Tellers guessed that the people on whom she modelled her characters died and she felt responsible for their demise. But they did not know everything. There was somebody there who noted the correlation between her fiction and reality and he wanted her to do a 'real' job for him: kill somebody through her writing. This person was stalking her. To stop it, Emma signed to 'Real Thoughts.'

An Escapist

Katy was a fashion model and several years previously she was on her way to become a supermodel, but she lost her chance to reach the top of her profession when after the death of her husband in a parachuting accident she withdrew from modelling. She resumed her career recently, but was not working regularly and avoided the buzz of celebrity life. Her almost reclusive lifestyle, however, made her appearances the more intriguing. Katy was not only more successful, attractive and better off than the rest of the group, but unlike them, she did not harbour any grudges to specific people. She was completely free of envy, and revenge was for her an abstract concept. And yet, she was also sorry for herself. This was because by the time Katy had her twenty-fifth birthday, her life looked like a generic biography of a famous model. When she was fifteen, she was discovered in her town by a modelling scout in a shopping mall. Next year she moved to London, two years later to Milan, where she joined a famous modelling agency. There she started dating a well-known actor, later a sportsman and finally a businessman, whom she married.

Her relationship with a handsome millionaire was widely reported in the media that pondered on her fairy-tale life. And yet, paradoxically, it was couple of days before her wedding, when she started to feel as if she was not living her own life, but played in a film scripted by a second-class Hollywood scriptwriter. She tried to explain this state to Thomas, her fiancé, asking him to postpone their wedding till she regains her sense of autonomy, but he was unable or unwilling to understand her. He rather preferred if they divorce soon, than call off the wedding. And so they married and Katy played well the role of a happy bride, but in reality she was deeply frustrated and dreaming about disentangling herself from the situation.

Soon after Thomas started to talk about them making a baby. This was bad in itself as there is nothing more obvious in the life of a famous model than a child, fathered by a fellow celebrity or a businessman. Katy could not agree also because of her growing antipathy to her husband. Not that he was a bad man; he was just a shallow and predictable man, whose tastes and views were easily guessed by looking at his birth certificate and a bank account. Katy was certain that if Thomas had not married her, he would be married to another model or an actress and that if they divorced, his new wife would be younger than Katy. These thoughts made Katy so depressed that she spent several weeks in bed, suffering from something like gastric flu. She was vomiting so much that it felt as if she wanted to throw away not only the food stored in her guts but her entire interior: her old self. Perhaps she succeeded because when she recovered, she was transformed. Her body was weaker than before the illness, but her mind was stronger. From now on some of her thoughts stand out, not metaphorically, but literally - they had a contour and a shadow. Their bulkiness was reflected in her new manner of speaking. Certain phrases she was uttering in such a way that they came across as distinct units – a bit like a poem, which is meant to exist outside the normal flow of words and bring to life its own world. She started repeat certain phrases involuntarily, as if they had an echo. But few people noticed these changes. This was because, as she concluded, nobody listened to her carefully; they just looked at her and only heard what they liked to hear. When she wanted to get over with something quickly, for example when she negotiated a contract or talked to her husband, she was talking fast and smooth, as previously. Later she realised that during this period she was learning to divide her thought into two categories: the 'thoughtful thoughts' and the 'material thoughts'. When she accomplished this skill, she was able to return to her old manner of speaking. Her perceptions also changed – she started to see certain objects in isolation, disregarding their background. These were things which she was able to manipulate. Initially she did not choose them, they lend themselves to her will. With practice, however, she learnt to affect reality by the power of her thought. She could be a good fairy, like Amelie from the famous French film, but opted for putting people into trouble. 'Why?', asked Emma, more with admiration than repulsion.

There were two reasons for it, explained Katy. One was that doing a charitable work is an intrinsic part of a 'celebrity package'. Nothing is more clichéd than a model or an actress touring orphanages or refuge centres and it was a routine which Katy wanted to escape most. Second, she was yearning for a real spectacle, one which is not rehearsed and not taking place in a controlled environment of a theatre or a television studio. 9/11 was the greatest experience of her life and she would gladly go to hell to see something like that again. But she knew this was not easy. She started employing her new found power by causing mischief at the catwalk. She put invisible obstacles on the road of the fellow models and waited for them falling over them. First somebody just had a wobbly walk, and later the models started to fall over in reality and several twisted their legs. This epidemic of accidents prompted journalists to write about the danger of high heels. For a moment high heels even went out of fashion, before they returned with vengeance, following Katy's boredom with this trick. After that she tried plane crashes, but this did not work. Her power had obviously its limits. Katy realised that this failure had to do more with the physical and mental proximity to the event and less with its scale. A proof to that was a hailstorm which took place in late spring in the village where she and Thomas had their summer house, destroying the plants in the manicured gardens of the villagers. This was the closest to 9/11 she could go, as far as spectacle was concerned. However, this beauty of destruction was followed by the tedium of rebuilding what was destroyed, as the villagers decided that they should work together to make their gardens and the whole village even more beautiful than before and everybody was rounded to plant new flowers in the cheerful 'friends of the Earth' atmosphere. Katy had to be part of it, as not to give the impression that she welcomed the apocalyptic weather.

Her last adventure was 'killing' her own husband in the parachuting accident. But this made Katy only miserable as his was not a spectacular death and this reflected on Katy's laziness rather than her mischief – it was easier to kill Thomas, whom she never really loved, than divorce him. After that she realised that whatever she achieves with her thoughts will be unsatisfactory, because it will be predictable, even more predictable than if she was deprived of such power. She came to conclusion that the only thing which could make her alive again was to meet somebody with similar powers who would try to affect her with her or his thoughts, in the same way she affected other people. If this meant dying, then be it. And so she started searching the web and found 'Real Thoughts.'

A Healer

The last person who told his story was John, the founder of the group. John was a psychiatrist, who worked with people suffering from schizophrenia, multiple personality disorders and other serious mental problems. His job soon turned out tedious because limited to prescribing drugs to patients, as it was assumed that they could not be cured, only made innocuous. To make his work more interesting, he started to check his patients' background, trying to establish whether something specific triggered their illness. He discovered that a significant proportion of them in childhood or early youth were faced with a task which they could not fulfil. Of course, we all face such situations, but in their case the pressure to 'climb the mountain' was so high and the resources to achieve this goal so low that they reacted to the circumstances by creating a private universe, in which they could hide and find an answer to their problem. Their solution was thus epistemological, not ontological. Again, this is not unusual as we all have dreams in which we are more beautiful and successful than in reality. But in their case the dreamworld took over the real world; they believed it much more than they believed in what was around them. However, most of people of this kind turned out to be still unhappy and John was wondering why: was it because the real world interfered with the invented world or because their dreamworld replicated the real world? This could lead to an interesting project of trying to make these people happy not by bringing them back into the real world, but by manipulating their invented worlds in such a way that these worlds functioned well. Unfortunately, his colleagues at the hospital did not share his interests and some objected strongly to his ideas on moral grounds, claiming that people should be brought to the material reality at all cost. This 'Matrix argument' did not appeal to John, as he always thought that blue pill is infinitely superior over the red pill, because happiness is not only more satisfactory but indeed more real than truth. Happiness remains the same; truth has to be adjusted to the new contexts. It is not good to be a Copernicus among people who believe that the Earth is flat or an Einstein in the company of the Plancks and the Heisenbergs.

Eventually during a congress of psychiatrists John met a colleague from San Francisco, named Maggie, who also thought that the key to happiness was a fit between reality and its mental image. She told John that she observed a new mental disorder on the rise, which she called the 'omnipotence syndrome'. It occurred when people attributed themselves responsibility for various events in which they did not participate, such as causing or preventing terrorist attacks. She told him that on the whole this lot was more socially adjusted than the type he dealt with. They did not need to be locked up and typically they themselves searched for psychiatric help, often not knowing if they had super-powers or only imagined them. Some of their stories were so well constructed that it was impossible to dismiss them. Even more bizarre was that some of their predictions turned out to be accurate. For example, Maggie asked a man who attributed himself a responsibility for two plane crashes to cause an extra aviation incident for her. He replied that he would do it in a way that would be practically harmless, and two days later a plane was in flames in Las Vegas. Maggie asked John: 'If there can be epistemological solutions to real problems, as in schizophrenia, then why they cannot be ontological solutions to epistemological problems as these people described? After all, what we observe in reality are only chains of events, not connections between them. These connections always take place in our heads, as David Hume or some other philosopher demonstrated. The whole point is to argue them well.'

John did not know how to respond. Although he did not regard himself as a straightforward realist, he still could not force himself into believing in people destroying planes from the distance by their willpower. So he set up this group - to find out how the most intelligent of crazy people narrate their lives.

'This is a bit dismissive of us', said Robert. 'We did not know we meet here to quench your curiosity.'

'I'm sorry', said John.

'I don't mind', said Katy. 'I do not mind to be investigated. On the contrary, I welcome it, as I would like to understand what is going on with people like us.'

'We are the avant-garde', said Les, the computer programmer. 'The history of humanity is the history of inventing lighter and lighter tools which can be operated from the greater and greater distance. Computer and the internet can be seen as the breakthrough in this respect. But why should we stop on the computer? Thought itself, trained in a special way, will be the ultimate tool. What you were talking here is how you trained your thoughts to be as effective tools as the old tools: be the new remote controller. We do not understand yet this process, but this is not unusual. People often invent something before understanding how it works. Here we try to understand.'

'Why our thoughts are so effective only if they are negative?', asked Robert.

'I'm not sure, but certainly the most spectacular inventions were always in the military industry. Take the internet', replied Les.

'What next for us?', asked Emma abruptly.

'Now is a time for you to convince me that you are miracle-makers by changing my life', said John.

'Are you not afraid of us after all that we told you?', asked Robert

'I am, but I'm also thrilled to be part of this experiment', said John. 'We are making history here, my friends'.

'How should we proceed?', asked Emma.

'It is up to you, you can draw straws, choosing one of you as an executor or do it together. Of course I do not expect you to involve me in your plot. It has to be a surprise. Hence, I suggest after today we part company', said John.

'Do you want to give us a deadline?', asked Les.

'What about one year?', suggested Robert.

'If this is meant to be a surprise, better avoid any deadlines', said Emma.

'Okay', said John.

'For me this whole thing is too predictable. I don't want to be a part of it', said Katy.

'So you won't be', said Emma with a smirk.

And so they parted company. For the next several months John was expecting that something strange would happen to him. But nothing happened. The planes he boarded reached their destination; the lifts did not stop between the floors and there were no terrorist attacks in his proximity. Neither did he experience anything particularly pleasant or uplifting. Eventually he started to be ashamed that he treated the stories of the Sorry Tellers so seriously. And yet, he often felt as if somebody observed him. He knew that this impression came from his head but this was a meagre consolation. The feeling of being observed was at its strongest when he was in his apartment, perhaps because the Sorry Tellers met there couple of times. His anxiety increased when he found in the newspaper an information that Katy was found dead in her house. The police described it as a suicide, but was unable to attribute her death to any specific cause, such as drug overdose. John tried to contact Robert and Les, to find out if they knew more about this accident, but neither was available. Their e-mail addresses no longer worked and they both changed jobs in the meantime. Emma he did not even try to trace, knowing that she did not give them her real name.

All this made John uneasy and prompted his decision to move to the States, where he looked for job offers for some time, indeed even before he set up the 'Real Thoughts' group. This time he put his thoughts into action. Eventually everything was arranged. John found a job on a psychiatric ward in San Francisco clinic and after some months of living in a rented accommodation he moved to a two-bedroom apartment in a newly erected block of flats. He was one of its first tenants. Everything there was super-modern, including the key. It was an electronic one, although more sophisticated and multi-functional than those one gets in the hotels. It was really a remote controller for everything in the apartment. Gas, electricity and water had to be switched on by using this key and windows also could be opened manually only after they were electronically unlocked. This way the apartment was practically burglary proof, which was a matter of great importance in security-obsessed America. John asked the man from the company who handed him the key what happens if the key stops working and he replied that there was another key kept by a concierge downstairs and, of course, the company would change the faulty key within an hour upon phoning the emergency number, which was printed on the emergency key. John was also assured that it never happened on this estate. The system was checked and worked well as more and more new houses operated this way.

It took some weeks to move John's stuff from England and prepare the apartment for his needs. To do so without stress, he took three months of leave and he still had almost month till his work started; he wanted to spend them on travelling in California, including visiting Maggie, who was now living in Los Angeles. Eventually his essential belongings were in a new place and he arrived with bags of groceries to spend there his first night. John put the key in the socket to switch on the electricity. But it didn't work. What a nuisance! He tried several times but without success. He tried to go out to let the concierge know about this problem, but the door was locked from inside and he could not open it. He tried to phone, but his mobile phone run out of battery and he could not catch an internet connection on his laptop which was, besides, also low on electricity. He shouted 'Hello! Anybody there? I need your help!!', but there was no response. He must have been the first tenant living on this floor, so not surprising that nobody could hear him. Besides, the walls were very thick. It was meant to be a block for people who did not want to hear their neighbours.

John started to feel thirsty and went to the kitchen, but water did not run because it also depended on the functioning key. Luckily he bought some orange juice and poured himself a glass. But he did not really like it; he only bought it because he could not buy his favourite 'Innocent' smoothie and the Americans must have had put extra sugar in it. Drinking it made him even thirstier. Soon it was dark. Lying in bed he was thinking about 'The Vanishing', a film about a man, who wanted to find out what happened to his girlfriend who vanished, and the only way turned out to be to vanish the same way as she did. He was not sure why he was thinking about the film – maybe because his flat started to resemble him the box where the characters were locked or because he also realised that his predicament was not an accident. He had problems falling asleep, but when wake up got more energy. He tried the key again, cried for help and examined the doors, walls and windows. In films set in prison there are always people who manage to make tunnels, no matter how thick the walls. But he did not even know where to start – which wall to attack and with what tool. He ate very little, knowing that eating will increase his thirst which will be much worse than hunger. Another day and night passed and another one and another one, and he started to be feverish. Most of the time he had no energy to do anything, so he did not feel bored and had no desires. It was worse when his awareness returned and he did not know what to do with the time he had left. He was thinking that it will be so much better if he had his books with him. And then he noticed a book lying on a small table in another corner of the room. It must have been left by one of the workers renovating the apartment. He tried to leave his bed, but had no energy and fell on the floor. From there he managed to see its title: 'The Sorry Tellers'.

Flowers of My Friends

It is assumed that all women love flowers, but typically it means that they enjoy receiving them from men who are in love with them. However, the women I have in mind never cared much about receiving flowers from men and, if they did, it wasn't enough; they wanted to be masters of their flowers. I also wanted to fall into this category, but it didn't work out that way; even cacti dried out and died under my care. Hence, I stopped cultivating my own pot flowers and then even buying cut flowers as I realised that this amounts to supporting the 'flower slaughter industry'. Currently, I admire flowers almost exclusively via intermediaries. Two such intermediaries I hold in my memory most vividly because, in their cult of flowers, they went further than anybody I know. At the same time, their attitude to flowers couldn't be more different from each other.

Lena or My Flowers Are Enough

The first was my Austrian friend, Lena. Lena was a singer in a band named Lost, first consisting of three and then only two members. The band gained some popularity in their country in the 1990s before quietly sinking into oblivion; this being except for a handful of fans who, myself included, made up for Lost's wider recognition with their utter devotion. I was especially haunted by the mermaid voice of the singer. Although I did not perceive myself as the groupie type, I wanted to learn who was behind the voice and the lyrics which were, true to the band's name, about loss, harm, and disappointment. There was defiance in Lena's voice, as if the siren wanted to persuade her followers that suffering loss was a gift, but not because 'what does not kill me, makes me stronger', as in the Nietzsche aphorism, but rather because 'what kills me, gives me immortality'.

After several failed attempts to contact Lena, I got her e-mail address from one of Lost's most devoted fans, although accompanied with a warning that she would be unlikely to reply. Days and weeks passed without any response and eventually I stopped waiting and had even forgotten that I'd written to her. But then, as it often happens to me, when hope is lost, the dream comes true and Lena replied, although only to tell me that she had nothing really to say about the band and her old life as a singer.

She moved on, had a different job and different interests. But I replied that I didn't mind and wanted to meet her anyway. She agreed, although with numerous conditions attached such as; I couldn't bring anybody to our meeting; that she would have only one hour for me; and that we would meet in a place of her choosing. None of these conditions were difficult to fulfil, so I agreed but, due to my work, the meeting could not take place for the next half a year anyway. In the meantime we started to write to each other with great intensity, on occasions exchanging three e-mails per day. Practically as soon as she decided that I deserved her trust, Lena started to send me photographs of flowers. There were several interesting things about them. First, the flowers were never placed against any background – they filled the entire photograph and it was tempting to conjecture that she didn't want to contextualise them; they were meant to remain timeless and placeless and most likely she expected the same attitude from the recipients of these photos. I thus refrained from asking her where she had taken these photos, although I assumed that the shots came mostly from Augarten, Vienna's famous Baroque public park, because she'd written that she lived nearby and had described her walks there. Second, the flowers were never young, always mature; as if they were a metonymy of the photographer who, by this point, was in her late forties. She also sent a series of photos of old and withered flowers. These were most likely from Vienna's main cemetery, the Zentralfriedhof, and there was something ethereal about them. Like Lena's singing, they invited one to follow them or enter them, as if they were the mythical vaginas dentatas or abysses, concealing their caverns behind delicate yellow or pink petals, on occasion folded like pillows and quilts made of silk. I couldn't miss the horror vacui.

By the time we met for the first time, I had over a hundred photos of Lena's flowers and was about to start to catalogue them, as if in anticipation of the moment when I would write about them. Our first meeting was in a café near Augarten, one of those where patrons are allowed to smoke as Lena was a heavy smoker; a trait which I admired given that most middle-aged women I knew boringly obsessed about their health and appearance. Because I'd seen her on the covers of Lost's records and a couple of their videos available on YouTube, it wasn't difficult to recognise her. This doesn't mean that she hadn't changed from how she looked in those twenty-year old videos. On the contrary, she had changed a lot; in essence losing her former good looks and becoming old and haggard. However, the process of aging sharpened everything that was distinct about her, such as her narrow and slightly hooked nose, her high cheekbones, and long fingers. Gum disease and many years smoking had made her teeth dark, crooked, loose and protruding, as if they wanted to escape from her mouth. When she wasn't talking she kept her mouth compressed, which gave her a severe look. The mermaid had changed into a witch and this was fine by me, as I regarded it as the natural trajectory of a mermaid.

We had a meal for which she paid half the bill, as she was careful not to owe anything to anybody, even – or perhaps especially - her fans. Then we went to Augarten. It was late May, the wonderful period when even the pessimists cannot argue that summer is coming. There were plenty of flowers in the park, but Lena, as for the flower lover she presented herself to me, was surprisingly inattentive. It was me who had to stop her, when I noticed a particularly beautiful plant to draw her attention to. After the walk we went to a café and drank wine. She told me more about her life and her disappointments: her reckless mother who gave birth to her when she was only sixteen and then left her in the care of Lena's aunt (her father was so absent in her life that she even didn't mention him); the lovers who abandoned her, on occasions for men; and girlfriends, with whom she parted upon discovering they had nothing in common, her being a rebel and them being conventional. Her story was that of a shrinking social world and eventually gravitating in on oneself; a kind of big bang in reverse. I realised that this contraction of her world was documented best in Lena's final record which included the song 'My Flowers Are Enough', her spinster manifesto, which listed all the things the protagonist banished from her life or never had: children, lovers, pets, a house (as opposed to a rented flat) for the glory of being locked in her ivory tower.

Although Lena had scheduled our liaison to last only an hour, we spent half the day together, eventually parting at the metro stop near her apartment, slightly drunk. The next day I had some other business in Vienna and then returned to England without visiting Lena in her rented 'ivory tower', because she didn't invite me there. We repeated this routine twice or three times. I enjoyed our meetings, although on the last occasion we were slowly running out of topics and, at the same time, we had failed to reach the stage where we were comfortable to sit and say nothing, maybe because restaurants and cafés do not lend themselves to sitting in silence.

I would never have seen where Lena lived, were it not for the fact that on my last visit I had an accident – I tripped on a protruding slab of pavement and hurt myself. Blood was pouring from my knees, my hands and my face, and all this happened practically in front of Lena's block. It felt like she had no choice but to take me in there and dress my wounds. We climbed to the fourth floor, me hobbling behind her as she strode resentfully ahead, and then entered her small abode – a one-bedroom apartment with an extra room fulfilling the function of a dining and a living room. It was neither as small nor as shabby as I expected, but it was weird. There were many flowers there, but all of them were dry, with their heads hanging down, as if they were convicts who died after a long torture. What shocked me even more was that, contrary to the impression she'd given previously, she did not grant her flowers autonomous existence, but used them to decorate her numerous photographs, ranging from the time she was a teenager to her most recent incarnations. This was like in Henry James' 'The Altar of the Dead', except that on this occasion the supposedly Dead was still alive and it was Lena. With my internal eye I saw the next stage – Lena lying there in a coffin, covered by these dead flowers.

Shortly after this visit our friendship dissolved. She stopped replying to my e-mails which, by this point, I was sending out of duty rather than pleasure, and she told the man who put us in touch that she found me boring.

Aga or Where Have All the Flowers Gone

It came first as a surprise to me that my friend Aga, who, like myself, was Polish and came from £6dŸ, got interested in flowers in her early fifties because, before she reached this age, she had many opportunities to learn about plants. This was because Roman, her ex-husband, had a gardening business and he used their apartment as its extension. He kept seeds there and experimented with plants, crossbreeding flowers and creating miniatures so that they'd fit in minute glass containers, not unlike a ship in a bottle. He was always on the verge of some botanic discovery, which was meant to bring him a fortune, but this never happened, at least not before Aga and Roman divorced.

I realised that Roman's job, rather than make Aga love plants, put her off them – they reminded her of a man whom she wanted to get rid of from her life. More time had to pass before she was ready to embrace them because, after the couple split, Aga got herself two cats who turned out to be extremely disruptive. They trashed everything that got in their way and they were particularly vicious to anything which they found on the windowsill, a portal to their freedom. It was only when one cat was killed by a car, when he jumped out to the street from the window, and the other died from cancer that Aga started to think about different companions. Initially, she bought several pot plants, some violets, one orchid and miniature chrysanthemums; the last not even for keeping but to take to the grave of her parents. Yet, once she put the pot of chrysanthemums next to the violets and orchids, she lost the will to part with them, thinking that it wasn't the fault of the chrysanthemums that they were regarded as more suitable to cemeteries than balconies. She kissed the small yellow-brown flowers, whispering: 'I won't let you go,' and put them on the windowsill in her bedroom between the violets and the orchids, as if to prove that chrysanthemums were of the same stature as orchids. And so Aga's story as a rescuer of flowers began. Soon she started to visit florists, asking if they had any spoiled pot flowers. The florists initially treated her with suspicion, thinking she was a tax collector or a waste inspector, or at best an eccentric to be avoided, but most agreed to give her the waste as it obviously meant less waste for them to dispose of. She took the plants home and tried to reanimate them, initially using water and potions for plants bought in the flower shops, till she elaborated her own formula using, among other things, her hair and nail clippings mixed with compost, on the premise that these fragments of the body are particularly nutritious. When Aga put the flowers in special trays, she stroked the leaves of these semi-dead creatures. If they delicately vibrated under her fingers, it meant they were on the way to recovery.

Most of the plants brought from the florists she managed to rescue. But it wasn't enough for my friend. Her next destination was the cemetery. There, the fate of flowers was even worse than those at the florists, especially after All Saints' Day when the cemetery attendants threw flowers onto a gigantic heap, together with used containers for candles, plastic bags and other grave decorations and soil. When Aga looked at the discarded plants she thought about the piles of bones from crematoria in films about the Nazi death camps. The flowers were like these anonymous remnants of people, deprived of their individuality and dignity, except that not all were dead. In fact, the majority of the pot flowers thrown away were still alive; people got rid of them because they didn't want to look after them. So Aga picked them out, put them in her small car, and brought them home to resuscitate them and nurture them to full health. For those which were dead, she tried to offer a more dignified place for their last rest, burying them in the back of the cemetery or in the allotments of her neighbours.

Eventually Aga had so many plants in her two-bedroom apartment, that there was barely enough room for her bed. She needed to move to the next stage. She set up a website: 'Pot Flowers Looking For Loving Homes' and so people started to come to her for free flowers. In common with the owners of pet shelters she was, however, careful not to entrust her plants to those who might neglect them. For this reason, she always asked the people whom had been gifted the flowers, to send her their photographs of them and return them if the plants got ill. Her visitors were almost exclusively women or men who wanted to give the special flowers to their wives and girlfriends, to prove that they were the 'caring type', who would rather get a mongrel from the shelter than an expensive pedigree dog. Such requests from men, Aga typically ignored. However, one day a man in his mid-fifties named Ryszard came, telling her that he wanted a pot flower for himself, ideally one which would keep him company till the end of his life, and one which had just one flower as he didn't want to be overwhelmed by beautiful creatures. It was not difficult to conjecture that he was both divorced and prejudiced against women, and that his relation to a flower would be sexual. Aga did not mind any of these traits, as she was prejudiced against the opposite sex herself and felt that the guy wasn't a rapist, but rather a stalker type and a caresser, and flowers like to be stalked and caressed. However, she told Ryszard that she was unable to fulfil his request in full because no plants flower continuously whilst, at the same time, have only one flower. Demanding from the plant to have just one flower would be like asking a woman to stay forever young and childless.

In the end she gave Ryszard a plant which looked like a bee orchid, except that it wasn't pink and brown but yellow and dark-red and, obviously, it wasn't a wild flower but one which was cultivated. Aga found two of those on the rubbish heap at the £ódŸ cemetery and had spent a lot of time and effort bringing them back to life, so it was hard to part with any of them, but she trusted its new carer. She assumed that she would never hear from Ryszard again but, not only did he sent her a new photo of the orchid every week which he called 'Aga's Bee', after some months he returned, asking her to give him another pot flower. This time she gave him some miniature Japanese irises. Normally they would be planted outdoors but Polish florists, seeking innovation at all cost, tried to miniaturise many flowers so that they could be sold in pots. As a result, a lot of flowers were discarded, leading Aga to fill her apartment with these crippled, diminutive creatures and posting online petitions against miniaturisation of flowers and plants at large (pun intended by Aga). In this way she joined in the anti-Bonsai movement and once, when visiting, I tripped on a pile of leaflets explaining – as I later learnt - in graphic detail what the plants suffer when they are not allowed to reach their full size, comparing their miniaturisation to the cruel practice of bandaging the feet of Chinese women. Only, on this occasion, not only are the feet of plants constrained but their entire bodies. Reading these leaflets, I couldn't help but think about Aga's ex-husband's attempts at plant miniaturisation. Was Aga not bothered about his experiments or was this a factor in their split? But I didn't ask her as she didn't like to talk about that stage of her life.

Subsequently Ryszard took a third pot flower from Aga, a yellow zebra plant. And then a fourth, a Christmas cactus as it was January and the florists were getting rid of unsold stock. On this occasion Ryszard mentioned that the number of his pot flowers matched the number of the women he had divorced. However, he kept visiting Aga, usually at weekends as on weekdays he was very busy with work, and started helping her in the shelter and going with her to the places where she expected to find her 'crippled orphans'. He would also bring her bags of shopping and invite her to restaurants, not least because Aga was so involved with flowers, while also working full-time, that she barely had enough time to eat (I guess she also felt guilty devouring the cousins of her beloved creatures). Eventually Ryszard invited her to his house. Reluctantly she visited him in what turned out to be a large house in Zgierz, a suburb of £ódŸ renown for a number of so called 'Gypsy palaces'; highly ornamented large houses with dome-shaped roofs and large external stairs, wide at the bottom and narrower at the top. Apparently, at one time, these buildings - erected in the 1980s - belonged to the most sought-after contract killers in Europe but, by this point, they stood abandoned and in disrepair. Ryszard told Aga that he had recently bought one of these palaces, as they were incredibly cheap, and he thought about using some rooms and the garden as a house for Aga's flowers. A greenhouse was also on offer. In the longer term, he wanted to make the Gypsy palace look like a kind of Xanadu from 'Citizen Kane', only lighter, more airy, and flowery. Ryszard assumed that Aga would be over the moon with his proposal but she, by this stage in her life, being practical, pointed out to him the various shortcomings of this solution to her problem. First, it took ages to get to Zgierz in the frequently heavy traffic so, looking after 'his flowers', would require her putting more money and time into her flower-rescue operation than she could afford. Second, for most of those who wanted flowers from her shelter, it was easier for them to get to her apartment in the centre of £ódŸ than from Zgierz. Thirdly, what would happen to the flowers if Ryszard changed his mind and decided to sell the house? Would he throw the flowers away like the florists or the cemetery attendants?

Ryszard then admitted that he also had plans for Aga. He wanted her to move there with him and become his fifth wife, if she were not averse to this bourgeois institution. But Aga refused. In principle, she didn't object to being somebody's fifth wife, but she didn't find Ryszard attractive. The long years of communing with the most beautiful creatures made her averse to the mousy-haired - or balding - square-faced and stout creatures that were to be found walking the streets of Polish towns, Ryszard included. She also felt that, despite superficially sharing a love for flowers, they had little in common. Yet, she didn't want to admit these truths. Instead she simply said to him: 'My plants are enough. I don't want anybody else in my life'. After this rebuttal, Ryszard stopped visiting her so often, but they remained on friendly terms. Eventually he installed a different woman in his Xanadu palace. Aga didn't like her, so she didn't entrust this woman with her flowers.

Over several years, whenever I visited her during my trips to Poland, Aga would tell me about her flowers. Because I lived in England - and was so inept with flowers - I couldn't take any pots from her and neither would it be practical to bring any flowers for her to nurture to good health. What I did bring were songs about flowers as, after flowers, music was my friend's greatest love. She liked Lena's songs, although found her, and rightly so, somewhat morbid. Most of all, she liked a compilation of different versions of 'Where Have All the Flowers Gone', including three by Marlene Dietrich. When the line 'Girls have picked them every one, when will they ever learn?', she had tears in her eyes and I hugged her and cried too, I don't know if from sadness or happiness.

The Left Behind

Lea wasn't sure when she started to feel different, but probably it was in London, during one of the conference dinners, to which she was invited with other university guests, all coming from language departments. She found herself sitting in a corner with only one person sitting next to her, a Chinese man, who quickly finished his meal and left. After that she could move one place and sit next to a French woman, but she was immersed in a conversation with her countryman, to whom she showed something on her mobile phone. Lea didn't want to intrude and the strong orange light coming from this woman's phone disturbed her. She moved even more to the edge of the table to stay away from the light.

Lea herself didn't have a mobile phone on her as she hardly used it. This was because she preferred to have different equipment for different purposes. To take photos, she used a camera. To find a new place, she consulted first a traditional map and then she drew her own small map which she held in her hand when looking for her destination. Most importantly, however, Lea simply did not like the look and touch of smartphones. For her, a smartphone was like a cross between a grenade and a rodent, waiting for a right moment to blow one's hand or bite one's ear, therefore she normally left it at home and only took it when travelling abroad. Even then, she put it at the bottom of her suitcase, where it quietly run out of battery. Lea's smartphonophobia didn't go unnoticed. People asked her how she managed to survive being so 'disconnected'. When she explained, they gave her funny looks or with ironic smiles wished her good luck in moving against the tide.

A couple of weeks after the episode in the restaurant Lea noticed that most people's smartphones emitted an orange light and that when looked from a specific angle, the ears and hands of some of the smartphone users were also glowing with orange light, albeit much weaker than that which the phones emitted. She didn't share this observation with anybody, not to reinforce her reputation as an eccentric, but at home she took the smartphone away from Alex, her son, replacing it with an old model of a mobile phone and asked him not to use it, unless absolutely necessary. Since then she spent much time teaching Alex the skills one needed when one didn't have a phone, such as using maps and playing music from vinyl records and CDs. To make him keener, she told him that this was what she and her father used to do when they were young, long before Alex was born.

Alex was initially dismissive of this 'back to the old days' exercise, but later started to enjoy the time spent on the old devices or without any electronic equipment whatsoever, cycling with Lea to the neighbouring villages and having lunch in the old-style cafés. It was on such trips that Alex also discovered the orange light originating from the bodies of some guests. Unlike Lea, for him the light had a different intensity and shape; on some occasions Alex saw a glow, on others sharp rays piercing the air and reaching as far as the ceiling.

'The orange monsters try to find the best way to take over people's bodies and launch an attack,' he said to Lea, pointing out to her a particularly strong orange ray, which for her, however, looked like a fragment of a blurred rainbow.

'Shh, don't say that to anybody,' said his mother. 'People will take us for nutters.'

'But we're not,' protested Alex.

'I know, but as long as the rest of the world doesn't see the world the way we do, our perceptions are not valid.'

On one visit to the café some twenty miles from home, Lea noticed that light also emanated from Alex and it was green. When by chance he lifted his hand, sharp green rays crossed in the air with one man's orange rays. The man must have got a strong headache as a result as he buried his head in his hands and went to the waitress asking for Aspirin. For the duration of their stay the guests' smartphones stopped working. In consequence, some people left before they finished their meals and one went to the manager accusing her of creating 'white space' to force the customers to eat more. Lea and Alex found this accusation rather funny, but they kept quiet and left when there were still several customers, so they couldn't be identified as the culprits. After that they tried to avoid this café. Luckily it coincided with a beginning of a period of short days and heavy rain, followed by an unusually severe winter, which put Lea and Alex off from cycling. They were spending most of their weekends at home, reading books, listening to music and playing board games. They also hugged a lot and touched each other's hands. Although it was enjoyable by itself and the two were affectionate all of Alex's life, they felt that now there was more to it than cuddling, as every time their bodies touched, a refreshing coolness moved between them and they became more energetic. Without saying a word, they knew when it was happening and giggled when it did so.

When winter passed, many of the children in Alex's school got ear infections. It was attributed to a nasty virus which arrived in the North of England, together with the bad weather. Its peculiarity consisted of attacking only one ear, the right in the case of right-handed-children, and the left in case of the left-handed ones. It caused a burning pain and black discharge, which looked like ash mixed with saliva. The doctors didn't know what to do apart from give the children antibiotics and vitamins because they were not familiar with such an ailment. Alex was the only child in his year who didn't get the illness. He told his form tutor that this was most likely because he stopped using a mobile phone, but she laughed it off, saying that it was proved beyond doubt that smartphones were completely safe and the school was not a place to spread conspiracy theories. But during the same meeting she praised Alex for making progress in practically all of his subjects. In less than a year he moved from being an average pupil to the top of his class. Alex believed that this was not because he had gotten much better, but because the rest of his class had gotten worse, but he didn't say it as he didn't want to offend anybody.

Eventually the ear infections cleared up but the children emerged from the illness weaker. Most lost hearing in one ear and after some time, in the other, as well as their appetite and energy. A year after the mysterious illness only about a dozen kids in Alex's school were still able to hear and the school had to adapt to teaching all children as if they were deaf. The same pattern could be observed across the whole region; children got ear infections which debilitated them. Lea was surprised that the media kept quiet about this epidemic; the only sign that it was acknowledged was indirect; the health section of the BBC website heralded the lowering rates of child obesity in Lancashire and Yorkshire, and the area's drive to learn sign language, which was presented as a sign of the growing inclusivity of the British society, particularly the North.

Alex didn't mind using sign language at school, but this made him eager to return home, where he could chat with his mother in his usual noisy way, with talking being mixed with laughing. In fact, every day he came home anxious that Lea might also lose her voice because deafness and muteness had become more common also among the adult population. Quietly and gradually, sign language became the dominant language not only at schools, but also in the offices of all sorts of businesses and even the parliament. Rather than fighting to translate sound language into sign language, now those who weren't deaf demanded that the sound language was preserved in national institutions, but their plight was usually dismissed as bigotry.

The spread of deafness and muteness affected the way films and music were produced and consumed. There was a massive return to silent cinema. New films were made without sound; old films were subtitled or discarded if it was deemed unprofitable to subtitle them. The makers and distributors of these films argued that only now cinema fulfilled its promise of becoming a universal language – the century of sound cinema was a step back on the road to achieving this goal. There was also return to black and white films, as people were increasingly insensitive to colour, but here the resistance was stronger, especially from the arthouse directors' lobby who didn't want to lose their distinction from those producing commercial films. In music, the louder instruments got prevalence over the quieter ones. Drums and bass guitars dominated the stage, rendering acoustic guitars, pianos and flutes redundant. Despite such adjustments, there was simply less demand for music, and musicians filled the queues for unemployment benefits. Many became homeless. One could see them begging on the streets of Marston, propped by their silent guitars, to indicate that they were not ordinary junkies or weaklings kicked out from their houses by their girlfriends, but a nobler kind, like the victims of tsunamis or political persecution. The problem was that the streets were now full of such destitute ex-professionals, surrounding themselves by their now obsolete instruments and almost nobody paid any attention to them. Everybody in Lea's work agreed that it was only a matter of time before the university folk joined them, but for some strange reason this moment kept being postponed.

Lea, who was both charitable and a music lover, was spending a large part of her salary handing money to the begging musicians. Eventually, she offered one such musician, a young man named Daniel with a sunny face and large dark eyes, who turned out to be half-Cuban and half-Hungarian, a room in their house. She thought, perhaps irrationally, that as Daniel knew three languages, he might keep his voice longer than most people.

Daniel was happy to move in. He admired Lea's collection of Spanish books and conversed with her in this language. Sometimes Alex joined in, as the silence surrounding him outside home made him eager to learn foreign languages – something which he didn't want to do previously. Daniel also played board games with Lea and Alex and started to teach Alex how to play guitar and drums, even though previously music was Alex's least favourite subject at school, till it was quietly abolished due to the spread of deafness. For Alex's thirteenth birthday Lea bought her son not one, but two guitars and a drum kit, as they were now sold for pennies. Daniel also turned out to be very good in repairing things in the house and even making furniture. Like Alex, he was also chatty and in a short time Alex and Daniel became best friends. Every day Alex was checking if Daniel wasn't producing any orange light and when he contracted it (usually after trip to a shop or a local diner), Alex extinguished it through the touch of his 'green hands'. He confessed to Lea that he was doing it also at school, and after several of his 'healing sessions' kids were regaining some of their hearing and voice. Lea asked if the teachers knew about his power, but he said no – he was doing it discreetly, not out of fear of teachers, but in order not to be pestered by the whole school.

The growing deafness slowed communication as everything now had to be written down or conveyed by gestures. People also started to make more mistakes in their writing than they used to. At Lea's university the lecturers got special training to learn what the students intended to say when they wrote gibberish and mark their work according to the merit of their intention. However, many of those who were meant to teach them also experienced illiteracy of sorts and were unable to decipher either the text or its intentions. Consequently, nobody now wanted to show colleagues how they marked their students' work in order not to be accused of incompetence. The management recognised the problem as it was itself also plagued with it. The response was limiting direct communication to the bare minimum. In order to send an e-mail to an external institution, one had to receive numerous permissions and even writing to colleagues required vetting by the head of department and somebody from the HR. Lea began to wonder whether other employers adopted the same procedures, but it was impossible to find out, because employers everywhere were secretive about their practices.

As weeks and months passed, Lea's workplace became quieter, literally and metaphorically, as the people lost the will to write or gesture, as well as their voice. In offices she frequently saw employees scrolling a mouse on a blank computer screen with a vacant expression or moving their finger on the lower parts of their smartphone as if they were reading the Braille alphabet. They even didn't do it to pretend that they were working, as they didn't change their behaviour when their superiors came in. There was much talking about the change - the approaching change was the explanation and excuse for this stupor, because there was no point in investing one's energy in the present if the present was meant to be swept away any minute from now.

Eventually the change was about to happen: the company Pineapple decided to introduce to the market a new smartphone, the 'wordless'. The idea behind it was that people would send messages using a phone which would absorb the person's thoughts, edit them and pass them to their addressee. This soon to be universal telepathy was meant to be the fastest, cheapest and most effective way of communication ever invented. To transfer their thoughts properly, however, people would have to focus on what they wanted to say or otherwise the wrong messages would be delivered or they would be unreadable or get stuck in the thoughts-processing centres. One could image how dangerous such situation would be, if, for example, political and industrial secrets were passed to enemies. A wrong use would also lead to unnecessary use of electricity and e-waste. In short, there were meant to be great advantages from learning how to use the Pineapple phone well and disadvantages in resisting this great invention. Pineapple admitted that the new phone was a bit bulky, but all great inventions started like that. In due course it would become smaller and more convenient to use.

Lea's university signed an agreement with Pineapple to launch there a pilot project to assess the effectiveness of the new phone before the device was to be used commercially; the Training Unit was given the task of testing the new technology on its employees. The skill needed to master it was labelled the 'channelled mode of thinking' and it consisted of thinking one thought at a time and making sure this thought was directed to the right address: the student, the colleague, the manager or somebody external. Thoughts had to move quickly rather than occupy one's mind endlessly and be work-centred rather than private or random, as this is what working should be about – being at one's office not only in one's body, but also in one's mind. To participate in this test, the staff was to wear the phone during their working hours. It looked like a helmet, filled with thin cords which attached themselves to the nerves like tentacles of the octopus, except that an octopus has only eight tentacles while this helmet had hundreds. The tentacles were meant to collect the thoughts and send them to the processing centres which would edit them before passing them further, as well as prepare the statistics for the day, listing how many messages were prepared correctly, how many went adrift, how many stay in one place and the overall quality of intellectual work performed by a given person. Those who had a low ratio of correct messages were to receive extra support either from motivational speakers or yoga instructors. The former were to help the staff think fast and straightforward; the latter to assist them in concentration on useful thoughts and to clear their heads from 'dust'. People gossiped that the best way to pass this test, which presumably would determine one's continuous employment or lack thereof was to clear one's mind by a line of cocaine in the morning. The management must have found out about it as the next day the campus was plastered with posters about the dangers of drugs and warnings that being caught on using them equalled instantaneous dismissal.

'Can I opt out from this trial?' Lea asked a woman who was leading one of the pre-testing sessions.

'Why do you want to do that?' asked the woman.

'I would like to keep my thoughts private,' said Lea.

'Honest people have nothing to hide,' said the woman.

'They might want to hide this very fact, in order not be taken advantage of,' said Lea.

'This exercise is not about curtailing people's privacy or censoring their thoughts, but about working more efficiently and improving communication. This is how humanity develops – by changing the modes of communication. Once one mode ceases being efficient, another needs to be introduced. We are now on the threshold of the communication revolution, but to make it happen, we need to show commitment.'

'Can you explain me why the old mode of communication stopped being efficient? Why people can't speak or write correctly anymore?' asked Lea.

'This is an evolutionary thing. Certain organs regress or disappear when they stop being useful, like tails on monkeys when they developed into humans. Of course, there are always "dinosaurs", who keep their extra teeth or useless tails, even groom them as if they were a sign of their superiority. But they delude themselves thinking that they matter; they are irrelevant or even obstructive. It is in these organs where toxins accumulate.'

Lea wasn't convinced by this argument, which sounded memorised and recited, so there was no point to discuss it any further, especially as her interlocutor produced an above average amount of orange light, which made Lea almost dizzy.

'Returning to your question, I will have to talk to my boss. I will let you know as soon as I find out,' said the woman.

The following week Lea learnt that going through the training was not compulsory, but was essential for keeping her professorial job and salary. The alternative was to get re-deployed, either to the university catering services or to estate management, moving furniture and other stuff along with the robots. She decided to go to catering as she couldn't do heavy lifting. She was sad to tell Alex, as he was always proud that his mother was a professor, but it turned out that he wasn't too concerned. He said that they would manage even on her reduced wages, as they were used to modest living and thanks to working in the kitchen Lea was allowed to bring uneaten food back home. In fact, there was so much waste food these days, that the leftovers were enough for all three of them. The government boasted that the epidemics of obesity was finally averted, but in Lea's view it was less to do with the policies of public health or self-restraint, and more with the general lethargy enveloping the population.

Some of her new co-workers, like Lea, found themselves in catering because of their refusal to wear the gear provided by Pineapple. They made their choices for various reasons. A couple of union activists objected because they were politically-minded and didn't want their thoughts being censored; two lecturers from psychology because they were prone to migraines and dizziness and believed that the 'helmet' would trigger their illnesses. There was also a woman from the fashion department who refused this gear because she specialised in designing hats and regarded the headgear hideous and a threat to her job. They were all called the 'Left Behind'. It was meant to be a term of abuse, but their recipients embraced it. 'We, the Left Behind must stick together,' they said and they greeted each other by putting their hands on their heads, as if to show that nothing, literally and figuratively, was exerting pressure on their brains – they were their own masters. Lea looked at this budding symbolism with amusement, yet she succumbed to it, because she didn't want to be left behind even by the Left Behind. She wanted to belong somewhere, not so much for her own sake, as for Alex's.

Lea quite liked her new work, not least because half of the people who were working in catering weren't deaf and even when they were making wraps and sandwiches, they engaged in conversation. They also didn't mind speaking their minds. But even the most outspoken complained that 'speaking one's mind' didn't mean what it used to, because society had lost the ability to judge others' outspokenness. The language of most people had become reduced to the basics and such layers of linguistic expression as irony went unnoticed by its recipients.

One day after work Lea found in her pigeonhole a piece of paper inviting her to a meeting at the professor of neurosurgery's house, Eric, who'd been demoted to the campus' assistant gardener. He lived in a part of Marston that Lea had never visited before. There were about ten people when Lea arrived, mostly university folk, but there was also a woman who used to work at the council and got fired when she demanded that a quarter of the city become an internet-free area.

They started the meeting by introducing themselves and then Eric said: 'We're meeting here because we are concerned about the future: our own future and that of our children and grandchildren. We are called the Left Behind, but I believe that it is the rest of the world which is moving backwards, while we, at least, managed to stand still.'

'Why do you think so?' asked somebody.

'The people who surround us are gradually losing their senses. It started with hearing, but now it is also sight, smell, taste and touch. And with the loss of the senses, comes the loss of intellectual power, as it is the use of the senses which allows us to develop intellect, as John Locke observed as early as the seventeenth century. And when both the senses and intellect are impaired, the will to live also diminishes,' said Eric.

'We are told that the loss of the senses has to do with development of intellect. The more intelligent people are, the less they need their senses. Pure intellect is meant to compensate for these losses,' said a woman from psychology.

'I think this theory is false. Intellect is not autonomous – it cannot develop in the void,' said Eric.

'If this is the case, why all of this happens?' asked Lea.

'I'm not sure, but I believe that this has to do with the consequences of long-term exposure to substances used in computers and even more so, smartphones,' said Eric.

'What substances?' asked somebody whom Lea had never met before.

'I don't know,' said Eric. 'I am or rather I was a neurosurgeon, not a chemist, but I think it is not a single element, such as mercury, whose effect on the body is fairly well-known, but their combination. And because as many as 62 different types of metals go into an average smartphone, it is very difficult to say which combination is most dangerous. It might be copper and neodymium, gold and terbium, zinc and dysprosium or all of them. But even before this epidemic, I discovered that some smartphones emit an orange glow which has the power to penetrate one's body, like sunlight penetrating bodies of people who spend too much time sunbathing. Once it has moved under the skin, it slowly destroys what is there, like the mysterious virus we heard about last year. Has anybody noticed the orange glow?'

Lea, of course, knew it very well, as well as the green glow, but she didn't want to bring it up, at least not until the others did.

There was only one person who saw it, a guy from criminology who specialised in explosives. Correctly, he also noticed that the light took two forms: rays and an amorphous glow.

'Rays are for shooting, glow is for strangling,' he said in an impassive voice.

'Why can't the rest of us see it?', asked a man with very thick glasses, which made Lea giggle silently.

'It's possible that together with getting weaker, we lose the power to notice what happens to us. Ignorance is a means of putting up with loss', said Eric.

'So we are doomed?' asked the woman from the fashion department.

'I hope not. There were plagues in the past which decimated communities, but in the end these communities managed to survive.

Sometimes the epidemic simply went away; on other occasions a cure was invented, like antibiotics. Here it seems to me that the first stage to halt the plague should be to give up smartphones. Instead, what we see is Pineapple introducing a more sophisticated version, which uses all these rare metals, only in larger quantities and produces more orange light, which goes straight to peoples brains.'

'Why do they do it? Do they want to destroy us?' asked the ex-council employee.

'We cannot exclude that possibility, but I think it has more to do with a need to conceal the old flaws. Once everybody is using the new version of the smartphone, nobody will ask what was wrong with the old version. This is how technology develops. Who these days, apart from historians, ponders on the disadvantages of using a jenny or printing machines? But I think we need to resist the change because the new smartphone is more dangerous than anything previously invented. It is not like a new jenny, but a new guillotine.'

'Why is this scheme being piloted in England, rather than in the States, where the company has its headquarters or in China where most of the smartphones are produced?' asked a man who used to work in sociology.

'Good question,' said Eric. 'In fact the pilot schemes are running in these countries as well. England, however, was chosen, because here the gap between what the people think and say publicly was deemed the greatest and this is especially the case in Marston. The assumption is that if the English people can be trained to "say" what they "think", everybody can. But this is exactly the reason why we shouldn't allow this to happen.'

'What should we do?'

'First we should resist the experiment, not allow the orange light to penetrate our bodies and those of our kids. We also need to have our eyes open to people who might have developed anti-bodies, anti-rays. It is them who will show us a way out of this apocalypse.'

'How to recognise them?'

'I'm not sure yet, but I know that there are already people working on constructing equipment which would capture the orange radiation. The hope is that it will be able also to identify the benign radiation. Most likely its carriers, our saviours, will be young and for some reason have been sheltered from the orange light until they were able to fight it. We need to have them on our side and extract their secret.'

'Surely we cannot do it without their consent and that of their parents,' said Lea.

'Why shouldn't they consent when the saving of humanity is at stake?' asked Eric rhetorically.

'Maybe they want to be left in peace. Maybe their parents want them to be left in peace,' continued Lea, thinking that already she'd said too much.

'This would be very selfish of them,' said Eric.

On the way back Eric and his friend gave everybody a bunch of leaflets to distribute. Fittingly, they were printed on the old, yellowish paper which practically stopped being used some years previously and was quietly rotting in the rooms housing defunct equipment, such as photocopiers and scanners.

Its author, on behalf of the 'Resistance' asked that people stop using the helmets and 'regain their voice'. Lea threw them in a bin on the way to the railway station, which took her almost an hour to get to. She was thinking how Marston had changed since she started working there twenty-six years previously. On the winter day of her job interview she'd thought how she'd never seen as nice a place as Marston. All the shops were beautifully decorated: Debenhams, BHS, Marks and Spencer and dozens of independent shops. And over the next fifteen years or so all of them had gone. Only food shops remained but they were also decimated. Against the background of their disappearance, restaurants, pubs, hairdressers and beauty salons became more prominent and it stayed this way for a while until a new app helped people cut their own hair and they stopped going to restaurants because of the crowds of homeless people living in abandoned shops nearby.

Back at home Lea asked Alex and Daniel whether they attracted any unusual attention at school. They didn't.

'Okay, but don't agree to wear a helmet or give blood or saliva or anything,' she said.

Eric's predictions turned out right. Although still few people were able to see the orange light, in the next year belief in its existence became almost universal. This could be gauged by the ferocity with which the government and the established media rejected its existence as a conspiracy. 'There is no orange light,' was a message which appeared on the screens of computers and mobile phones, as well as on posters and billboards. Inevitably, as soon as such posters were put up, people got rid of the 'no'. Like in the past tattoo parlours became popular, now the cities were filled with shops selling meters measuring one's 'orange radiation', as well as measuring it on their premises. They were all illegal, but nobody cared – after many years of disappearing professions it was one which offset, albeit in a small measure, the losses of industry and trade. Soon the orange light meter sellers started to offer pills and tonics reducing the radiation. Again, the authorities warned against their ineffectiveness and toxicity, but this was seen widely as a proof that they were actually working. However, people were waiting for the true breakthrough – something which would allow them not only to slow the penetration of orange light into their bodies, but regenerate them.

One day Alex came to Lea's work to fetch her to see Daniel's gig. Paradoxically, Daniel started to get more work recently, not because people were regaining their hearing but because those who were still able to hear were looking for spaces where they could meet like-minded or rather like-sensed people. During the concerts people would often throw their arms forward. This was to show that no orange light emanated from their hands: there were no traitors among them. Lea was reluctant to do so, as she didn't like to participate in public displays of emotions. But, as the people around her looked at her, she did so and so did Alex. It was then that everybody noticed that they both produced more green light than the rest of the people in the room put together. Especially Alex – the rays from his hands managed to reach the furthest corners of the hall, changing the gloomy room into something like an old-style disco.

After the concert Lea and Alex were surrounded by the rest of the audience. The people asked Alex to touch them – their ears, the top of their heads, their mouths. Alex did as he was asked, and some people put money into his pocket as he was doing it. But that wasn't the end of it. He was asked to meet their relatives and friends. One woman said that she could arrange a large-scale 'healing session' in an old church.

Lea decided to intervene. She jumped in front of her son, saying. 'Please, leave him alone. He's just a boy and we don't need your money.'

Lea took the notes out of Alex's pockets and tried to give them back, but nobody accepted them.

'Keep them, keep them,' they were shouting.

They returned home by taxi. As they were leaving, people were stood by the wayside, waving to them. It appeared that there were more of them now than there were at the concert.

Back at home Lea said to Alex: 'We cannot stay in this city. If more people learn about your ability to produce green light, we will be besieged. Somebody might want to kill you to extract the light from your body. We have to escape.'

'Mum, we cannot run away. These are my people. If I don't save them, they will perish.'

Daniel joined in, adding, 'Alex is right. We have to stay here,' and he put his arms around Lea and Alex and Alex embraced Daniel and Lea. Lea also, somewhat against her will, stretched her arms out and put them around Daniel and Alex, so that they created a circle. Then Lea noticed that there was a second circle surrounding them, made of green light. It didn't stay still but moved as in a joyful dance.

The Less Intelligent

I often wonder what our ancestors were thinking when they embarked on the project of constructing artificial intelligence. Didn't it occur to them that such attempts amounted to an admission of not having enough intelligence? Or weren't they afraid that artificial intelligence would render natural intelligence redundant? These assumptions eventually became common sense. I was born at the time when the predominant view was that humans, or rather their descendants, lacked intelligence and that natural intelligence was superfluous. This view is held by our masters – the Intelligent. They no longer add 'artificial' to their description, because it presupposes 'natural intelligence' as a norm from which there are deviations. Such concepts the Intelligent reject; they see themselves as the norm and us as an exception – them being intelligent, us much less so.

We call the Intelligent the 'Ice' and we refer to ourselves as the 'Lice' or the 'Lies' (from the Less Intelligent, the LIs). Which spelling is correct, I'm not sure and there is nobody to tell me (I'm settling for 'Lice' as this word is easier to write). Not only do we lack linguists, but most are illiterate, so we don't care about spelling. Our language is made up of simple words, many of them based on acronyms, whose origins we have forgotten. To write the history of the Less Intelligent, I had to find these origins. Preparing myself to write this history took me a lot of time. However, the history itself will be brief; for two reasons. First, the history of the Lice is short in comparison with the history of humankind and all intelligent creatures living on Earth, and includes few important figures and events. Second, I'm writing with difficulty, so I'm trying to cut out anything which is not necessary.

I decided to start with myself, not because I am an important figure, but because describing myself reveals a lot about our history. My full name is Gerald 17.0906364. Gerald means that I was a child of Gerald (who was a female Gerald), and that the last known of my human ancestors also had such a name. The 17 at the beginning of my surname means that I belong to the seventeenth generation of the Lice. In a nutshell, this number determines my energy allowance (chiefly electricity) and other minor privileges. The higher the number, the lower the energy allowance; my allowance is about 2 per cent smaller than my mother's, but 1,5 per cent higher than the next generation after me. I was born on the ninth day of the sixth month of the year 364, which was 364 years after the end of the last war in which humans participated. Probably this was the Third World War, but I'm not sure – I know even less about the history of humans than I know about the history of Lice.

The year when this war was finished was hailed as year 0. The time before this event the Lice describe as BC (Before the Catastrophe), after – AC (After the Catastrophe). These terms were initially outlawed by the Ice, but using them was a form of resistance so the Lice were attached to this term. As by now most of the Lice have lost the memory of what C stands for (such long and negative words evaporated from our dictionary), they are now permitted to use them. Beginning at year 0, humans stopped being referred to as 'humans' and started to be called the Less Intelligent. First it was just a matter of semantics, but over the time it became reality. Currently, very few of the Lice are aware that humans were their ancestors and that they once ruled over the Ice; they are convinced that the Lice are a different species from humans, genetically engineered by the Ice, who arrived on Earth from a far-away planet, as the official history of the Ice has it.

You might think that the war which I refer to was between humans and AI, yet the situation was more complicated. It started as a conflict between adherents of two competing visions for the future of Earth. On one side were those who described themselves as the 'Greens'; on the other those who were described by them as the 'Polluters' or the 'Browns' and which included everybody who was not Green. The

Greens wanted re-greening of the Earth by such measures as a decrease in energy consumption and reduction of population. The Browns claimed that, however noble, these goals were impossible to fulfil without abolishing democracy (or what was left of it at the end of the 21st century) and making human life misery. They were in favour of leaving things as they were, hoping that the Earth would sort itself out, as it always did, apparently. They also pointed to the fact that things were moving in the right direction, from the Green perspective: the birth rate was declining; new biodegradable materials were invented, to replace the deadly plastic; most cars were electric and people had started to eat less meat.

Yet, this was not enough to appease the Greens, especially as, in addition to saving the Earth, they had an ambition to rule it. However, they couldn't win over the Browns in the elections, given that apart from preaching about the Apocalypse, they were largely absent of political ideas. But they had access to big money and, with it, they developed special robots called 'super-intelligent units'. The stated purpose of these machines was to help the governments to reach their 'green objectives', but the true goal was to defeat the Browns. A lot of money was invested in this project – roughly one third of 'free cash', patiently waiting to be put in motion, some three quadrillion American dollars. At some point these robots started to proliferate, as if of their own accord. They were running factories, concert halls and universities. They also made inspections in people's houses to give them instructions on how to live more efficiently, greener and longer - it was called 'Re-greening Stage 1 (RS1)'. If this did not work, they repeated their visits and then took the offenders to re-education camps, from which they did not return. Then they moved to the empty houses – it was called 'Re-greening Stage 2 (RS2)'. The Browns protested that the super-intelligent units did not lead green lives themselves. On the contrary, production and powering them was very costly, given that they were made from complex and rare materials, including copper, zinc, platinum and tungsten, as well as human tissue cloned and fortified in special labs ('human fortified flesh'- HFF) and they needed two types of nutrition: one to feed their human side and one their electronic form.

Such was the hostility towards the 'intelligent units' that gangs of young Browns attacked the factories which the intelligent units controlled and burned down the houses which they repopulated, calling it, provocatively, re-browning. There were also riots, organised by people wearing brown vests. However, such actions became more difficult as the years passed. There were heavy punishments for resistance against Re-greening and the population of Earth became more segregated, with the super-intelligent units and the Greens occupying the best quarters of the available space, and the Browns being locked in over-populated, squalid ghettoes. In the end the Browns lost and the Greens won, at least nominally. In reality, the victory was more on the side of the super-intelligent units than the Greens.

Subsequently, humans (the Browns because they lost, the Greens because they won) agreed to a programme of further containment of human power, of which the first step was evacuating certain areas, regarded as most vulnerable from the perspective of biodiversity and preserving the atmosphere, such as the Amazon and Congo rainforests. The next step was banning plastic or what was left of it, strict birth control, limiting each woman to two children (after the second child she was meant to be sterilised) and imposing limits on energy consumption. I think it was during this stage that the names changed – super-intelligent units became Is and the Greens and the Browns merged and became the LIs; and the words 'human', 'humanity', 'humanism' quietly disappeared from use.

When the population of the Lice shrank by half, which was about 100 years AC, the Ice determined that Lice did not need all the territory which they had at their disposal and it would be good to return some of it to other animals and plants. Given that the population of Australia and New Zealand was relatively low and- the cultural differences between inhabitants of these areas and the rest of the so-called western world were small, the Ice engineered the transfer of people living there to Europe. They were transported by ships because by this point airplanes were outlawed. (They remained in use by the Ice, though, for re-greening activities).

When, over time, the population of the Lice fell by another 30 per cent, the Ice decided to contain them on two continents: Europe and Asia. Eventually they were put in special zones, where they could, notionally, self-govern. They were called 'zoos'. A 'zoo' stands for the 'zone of opulence', because when the Lice moved there, they were told that they would find there everything they needed to be happy. The very fact of moving to the zoo meant that they could be catered for better than if they were spread all over the continents. The zoofication of the Lice lasted almost a century and in some ways it continues to this day. The remote tribes, such as Pygmies and other hunter-gatherers, who stayed away from the conflict between the Greens and the Browns continuing, instead, to live as they had for thousands of years, were initially meant to be spared relocation, in recognition both of their low environmental impact and that they would perish if put in contact with the Lice, not being immune to viruses carried by the larger more diverse populations. Eventually, however, it emerged that the Ice were unconcerned about human biodiversity and the Ice moved these populations into the zoos with everyone else and, indeed, they perished within a decade. Most from exposure to ailments they had no resistance to; some from what was understood to be broken hearts having been taken away from their homelands and ways of life. Before they died, they told our ancestors about the luxurious dwellings and labs being built in the rainforests and remote savannahs. Apparently it was also where the Brain and its entourage had its headquarters, but I will write about the Brain in due course.

For a couple of generations the old conflict between the Greens and the Browns was played out in the zoos and the Ice did not try to extinguish it, as it was another way to keep the Lice in check. However, eventually these old divisions ceased to matter, as everybody lived the same, standardised life. The vast majority of the Lice do not know or care to which political bloc their ancestors belonged. But I know, as my mother told me, that I am a descendent of one of the last leaders of the Browns; his name was Gerald Taylor - therefore my mother's name was Gerald and my name is Gerald. (The Ice, who weren't bothered about the difference between forenames and surnames, made forenames our default names).

There are no official figures – none that are available to the Lice anyway - about the current numbers of the Lice and the Ice but, according to my mother, in her days there were about 1.5 billion of us and 3 billion of them. A small proportion of Ice live around the zoos; these are the Ice of the lowest order. The rest repopulated the continents vacated by the Lice; with the highest classes living in the warmest and most pristine parts of the Earth, as the Ice like warmth and moisture much more than the Lice.

My height is 153 cm and my weight about 46 kg. I'm a quite a bit above the average height and weight of an adult Lice male of my generation. I believe I'm about 30 cm shorter and 30 kg lighter than an average male from the time when humans ruled the world. I'm 37 years old and I should die within the next decade and a bit. The reduction of weight, height and life expectancy compared to the days of the humans is a result of a combination of factors, of which the most important were malnutrition and diseases among the first generations of the Lice, living in zoos, followed by selective breeding, whose purpose was to make us smaller and lighter, and in this way make us consume less food. We also have less living space and our houses are standardised. The majority of the adult Lice live in three-storey blocks divided into twenty or so living units. Each unit consists of three rooms and each room is inhabited by three Lice. For every three rooms there is a kitchen and a bathroom. We managed to retain the right to a warm shower but its length was reduced over many generations and now it is five minutes long every third day.

Blocks are segregated by sex and age. There are blocks for neutered men and women. Mothers with children live in separate zoos, as do non-neutered men (they would be classed as sexually active, if they were humans). There is no contact between the zoos, because they are separated from each other by electric fences. It is assumed that such organisation ensures greater harmony and contributes to a more efficient use of energy.

For many generations now all Lice children are the product of artificial fertilisation. They do not know their fathers. Most male children are sterilised at birth; this is also my case. My mother says that there were two reasons for such a practice. One was the reduction of the population; the second was subjugation of menfolk. The communities of Lice were meant to be matriarchal; the gate of each zoo was adorned with a (somewhat faded by now and unintelligible to most Lice) sign 'Our Future is Green and Female'. I'm not sure about the first part of this sentence, but the second is certainly true. When a boy is born, it means that he will be the last in the line; he might pass his genes to his children, but nothing else: no values, no knowledge, no male jokes. Nowadays female Lice are also taller and heavier than male Lice and they are more intelligent. I, for sure, never met anybody as intelligent as my mother. I guess she would be regarded as smart even BC. Ironically, however, this female supremacy is not reflected in semantics – all Lice have male names, irrespective of their gender – being the progeny of some human male.

When a Lice child is born, he or she receives its full name which includes his or her expiry date – the maximum number of years she is allowed to live. The children are left with their mothers till the age of fifteen, as this is regarded as the most efficient and ethical way of bringing them up. When they reach this age, they are moved to the adult zoos and their connection with their mothers is severed for the rest of their lives. To ease the pain of separation, parents and children receive special treatment. It is popularly called the 'second neutering', although this is a pharmaceutical, not a surgical procedure and affects the brain rather than their reproductive function. The result is that after this procedure children do not miss their mothers and quickly forget them. They also do not develop either physically or intellectually. They don't grow, they lose their appetite, as well as curiosity and desire to change their lives. They do as they are told. I guess they became like the early robots – excluded from history, even their own.

For some reason, however, my body partly resisted the second neutering, as proved by the fact that I remember my mother well and I continued to grow till my mid-twenties; this is the reason why I'm so tall. I even have a nickname 'Gerald the Great'. I don't know why it happened this way – maybe my mother put something in my food when I was small or made me grow by my willpower. While mothers of other kids basically left them to their own devices, only teaching them how to dig up potatoes and carrots and peel and cut them to make soup or how to recycle the junk left by humans, she told me everything she knew about the history of our ancestors. The most important part of this story was that my last human ancestor – let's call him Gerald the Last Human - never reconciled himself with the defeat of the human race and believed that it would strike again. For him, this was only a matter of finding a new leader. He passed this hope to his daughter and she to her daughter and so on. At some stage one of these Gerald women came up with the notion that it would happen when the Gerald gave birth to a male, who would become the saviour of the Lice. The alternative would be the end of the Gerald line. This became a prophecy and they passed it from one Gerald to the next. When I was small, my mother told me that, along with the histories of various great human leaders and revolutionaries, such as Jesus Christ, Martin Luther King, Che Guevara and Luke Skywalker. But she failed to impress me as I pondered how, if they were so great, influential and victorious, why did humanity end up in such a perilous state. My mother was not able to give me a good answer– she told me only that it was probably because they were defeated by bad leaders. 'If they were so ineffective, why do you think

I would be any better, being just a dwarf with a hoe and hammer as my only weapons?' I asked and again. She wasn't able to answer.

At some stage we stopped talking about me becoming a saviour, as if she acknowledged that it would be unlikely. She even admitted that such prophecies were common in the early history of the Lice, but they died out together with males who were meant to be saviours, but ended up being weaklings like everybody else, just more frustrated than the rest of Lice folk. I don't know how many 'to-be-saviours' live in the zoos now, but there is one in my block. He is called John, is even taller than me and was fed with the same forecast. The difference between us is that he believes in his mission and acts according to the prophecy.

I shall add that even if a true saviour were born among the Lice, he would probably have to act alone because in zoos there is no appetite for revolution. The Lice are neither interested in their past, nor their future – they live in the present. The present-ness is inscribed in the organisation of the zoos, which are basically self-governing. We produce our own food and electricity from biomass and we look after our own people. We do not hoard any supplies because there is no point – nobody would buy them and they would rot if kept for too long.

The Lice are mostly vegan. Growing animals in zoos was outlawed on the grounds of it being too energy-intensive and immoral. The animals, which were kept for food by humans, such as cows, pigs and chickens, died out in our part of the Earth hundreds of years ago. John, however, claims that they are still kept by the Ice, but I cannot confirm it. There are also no birds, but some birds, such as magpies and starlings, apparently, were still flying over zoos less than three generations ago. Sometimes the Lice catch rats or squirrels and boil or roast them; this is treated as a major celebration. The Lice dance around the fire and sing songs. Technically this is forbidden, but the Ice indulge our small transgressions.

When somebody in the block dies, a young Lice takes his place so that no room is wasted. Among the first generations of the Lice this led to conflicts, because then different Lice represented different ethnicities and cultures. However, after less than a hundred years of zoos' existence, all these differences became obliterated. The current Lice know only one language (a simplified version of English), eat one type of food (fresh fruit and stewed or roasted vegetables), follow the same regime (get up at 7 and go to bed at 10), even dream the same dreams (in which they do the same things as in reality, albeit faster and with more grace).

The Lice do not travel, unless for pragmatic reasons. International and intercontinental business and tourist travel are obviously things of the past, given that there are no more nations, as well as energy-intensive means of travel, such as cars and planes. For travel we only use bikes, canoes, sledges and skies, depending on the weather and the place where we live. To communicate with each other, we talk. There is also a notice board at the centre of a zoo, where people can put up a notice addressing the entire zoo, but it happens rarely. On occasion, the Ice put up information for us, such as that we need to leave our homes temporarily, for essential renovations. Such announcements come mostly in the form of images, because of the high level of illiteracy among the Lice. The first generations of Lice, living in the zoos, were using computers, but they were abandoned, in part due to electricity restrictions and later because the Lice forgot what they were for.

When the Lice achieve their expiry date or when they become severely infirm (whichever happens earlier), they are brought to a special place at the outskirt of the zoo, where they are put to sleep by an injection, administered by one of the Ice of lowest rank. Their bodies are then used for harvesting HFF. The rest is put in a big hole where it disintegrates with the masses of other bodies, providing biomass, to be used to produce electricity. We don't entertain the concept of a burial, as such symbolic gestures are energy-intensive and, besides, our power of symbolisation is very limited. This is also how my life will end, most likely: as material to use for making spare parts for the Ice and generating electricity. I wouldn't mind if not for the fact that this would disappoint my mother.

Some of these rules, however, have exceptions. The previously mentioned John is one, because he passed his expiry date eight years ago, yet is allowed to live. He is also using a computer openly and got a special electricity allowance for it. John, like myself, came from the 'Lice aristocracy'. His ancestor owned the biggest technology company called Google. Also, like myself, he was told by his mother that the history of the Lice would end with him. However, unlike me, he took such prophecy seriously and believes that he will start a new epoch. His mission is to revive the old technology, penetrate the Ice's network and destroy it. John often comes to my room and suggests that we join forces for this purpose, but like most Lice, I'm interested in neither revolution nor computers. Many of the Lice believe that John is a spy; the Ice planted him in our community to check if we aren't plotting a revolt. I, however, believe that he is genuine, and that him being left to live as long as possible has to do with the Ice wanting to know what our current natural lifespan is, as John claims.

Messiah or not, I must admit that John is very intelligent. Thanks to his computer skills he is also able to find out some details about the Ice's history and about what they are up to. His version of human history also adds nuance and partly contradicts my mother's version. In particular, he told me that the real reason for the war, which wiped out humans, was HFF. This material was used to improve early robots, whose movements were jerky, touch lacked subtlety and faces were expressionless. HFF proved more robust than the normal human flesh and humans wanted to use it as well, to prolong their existence. However, this cloned material was very expensive and created a lot of waste. There was also a backlash against using it, especially given the overpopulation, climate change and the rest of it. Yet, this did not thwart the demand for HFF, only drove it underground. In the process, it was discovered that the highest quality of HFF was achieved by combining cloned flesh with naturally produced flesh of foetuses, umbilical cords and newly born babies. There was a time, John said, when thousands of newly born babies were snatched to prolong human life. The human governments were not able to deal with this problem, hence ceded it to the most advanced computer, whose machinations led to the Catastrophe and the creations of zoos. John told me that the need for HFF is the reason that the Lice females get inseminated and give birth and that the Lice still exist. Yet, something about a new generation of HFF recently went wrong, as proved by the fact that millions of Ice malfunction.

John explained to me that even when humans nominally ruled the Earth, artificial intelligence had a tricuspid structure. At the top there was the Main Processing System, currently known as the Brain or the God Father. It was the humans' loss of control over the Brain which sealed their doom. In John's words, the intelligence of humans and artificial intelligence moved in opposing directions: the former got more fragmented; the latter consolidated. When the Brain became independent from its human masters, its main objective became to further the interests of AI, rather than humans. The other part of the AI were the networks of intelligent software and algorithms, dominating the virtual space without a physical presence: the 'Holy Spirits'. Finally, there was AI embodied in robots, the 'super-intelligent units' who became the Ice.

Currently, the most important decisions about the Earth's governance are still made by the Brain, who passes them via the Holy Spirits to the Ice. Officially the transmission of commands is perfect, and the Ice and Holy Spirits feel blessed to live in utter harmony with their Father. However, according to John, the transmissions are not smooth. First, the Brain is ageing – he is unable to renew himself sufficiently and he lost much of his intelligence since he was created. Second, there is a discord among the Ice. This is because, although in theory each Ice is entitled to the same amount of energy and HFF, in practice the Ice trade between themselves these precious goods and the stronger individuals force the weaker to pass to them some of their HFF allowances in return for protection. Increasingly, there are gangs raiding labs where babies are delivered to snatch them for harvesting HFF.

The Ice are also divided into factions due to their conflicting views on sustainability and biodiversity. The default position of the Ice is that the main goal of governing the Earth is to preserve its natural resources, especially its biodiversity, for which the biggest threat is the proliferation of the Lice who, despite all these restrictions I described, are still the prime users of the Earth's resources and its main polluters. According to John, however, all the energy reductions imposed on the Lice were passed to the Ice and currently they use many times more energy than the humans in the last period BC. This is visible: an Ice is on average two and the half metres tall and their weight is over 200 kilos. They are fearsome figures and they know it. It is because of them that the Earth's temperature is going up and the icebergs continue to melt. But we are not allowed to check it or oppose it and even if we did, we lack the tools to do so. We are small, weak, and we have no weapons.

The most extreme position concerning the future of Earth is taken by the conservationists, namely those Ice whose main concern is conserving energy and the Earth's resources. They are in favour of total extermination of the Lice, regarding them as a cancer on the planet. They also argue that our extinction would solve the problem of crime caused by the fight for HFF, because this would compel the Ice to find a better method to manufacture substances needed for prolonging their lifespan. On the other end of the spectrum are the preservationists, who want to maintain or slightly expand Lice's population on the grounds that their further onslaught would cause degeneration or even an extinction of the Ice. For preservationists, the fates of the Lice and the Ice are connected. There is even a small fraction of the preservationists, who call themselves the Greens. These Ice Greens claim that the poor health of the Earth has little to do with the Lice, and all to do with the Ice. They advocate reducing the number of Ice, increasing the number of Lice and moving us from the zoos to open spaces where we can live free lives among other animals, such as birds, rhinos and lions. Then there are the moderate Ice of different political colouring, who are not in favour of total annihilation of the Lice, but of the reduction of our population by different measures and cutting our energy allowances. All lobby the Brain to agree with their positions, while the Holy Spirits, who can be compared to mischievous postmen, make up their own mind about which messages to deliver to the Brain and which take back to the Ice.

As there are so far few Greens among the Ice and the Brain dismisses their arguments, no doubt remembering what happened to the Browns when they were defeated by the Greens, the Lice are doomed. The question is only whether we will be slaughtered in one go or slowly harvested till there is nothing left of value to extract from us. Yet, contrary to what you might think, the bulk of the Lice are not troubled by the prospect of their extinction. Neither are they unhappy about their existence. My mother explained this by giving two reasons. One is the loss of intelligence, the return to the basics, to the soil. This means that there is no long-term planning, no cunning. For each Lice, every day is their entire life. This is in contrast to the Ice who are so consumed by achieving immortality that they are unable to live in the present and hence they need the whole eternity to start to live properly. And so they would never get immortality, said my mother with malicious satisfaction. The second reason why the Lice are reasonably happy is because there is little inequality in zoos, and inequality breeds resentment. Actually, at some stage the Ice started to be resentful about our serenity and therefore they introduced the rule of 'soft rules'. This means that in our world there are no absolute rules. For example, we get certain energy allowances, but some of us get a slightly higher allowance than the rest. We die at the same age, but some of us are allowed to live a bit longer. According to my mother, the rule of soft rules was meant to seed hope and resentment in our communities. But this purpose was not fulfilled. The Lice are neither hopeful nor resentful.

The same was true about me. I was thinking that all the knowledge about history that my mother tried to instil in me only led me to the conclusion that species come and go and the new dominant species does not care about the one which came before them. Who among humans lamented the demise of Neanderthals and Homo Sapiens? They enjoyed their heyday and then perished, giving way to humans, who were more adaptable and cleverer, similarly as humans gave way to the Lice and the Ice. They will also perish; maybe there is already a new intelligent form in the making: the Vice (the Virtual Ice) or the Mice (the Mega Ice). But then I got thinking that it will be sad if the Lice lack their own history, even if only a short one. Moreover, if I wrote it, the prophecy, which was passed to my mother and which she passed to me will be fulfilled, namely the *history* of the Lice would be finished when a guy called Gerald was born.

John, whom I told about my plan, became very enthusiastic and assured me that this history would be disseminated on paper, electronically and carved into the caves we have in our zoo. In fact, recently this carving became his main obsession; overtaking his passion for hacking. He elaborated a special pictorial language to translate my history into pictures and assembled a team of boys with whom he spends long hours, carving these pictures onto the walls of the caves. They've already covered about twenty metres of cave walls with pictures. The Lice like to do it and the Ice allow it, assuming that this is another sign of our regression, which was, after all, their plan, when they imprisoned us in the zoos. Probably they are right.